Troy swept Olivia into his arms. "Get back in the car!"

"Are you all right?" Her eyes were wild. "Tell me you're all right."

"Not until you're in the car." He shoved her into the backseat and dove in behind her, slamming the door behind him.

She held his face in both her hands. "You scared me half to death."

"I'll need to get this suit dry-cleaned for my brother. Other than that, I'm fine."

Her mouth pressed gently against his. His pulse was still racing. He was breathing hard. The extreme pressure of battle clenched inside him, tying his gut into knots. But the sweetness of her kiss did a lot to ease his tension. Every fight should end with a kiss from a beautiful woman as a reminder of what was really important....

MOMMY MIDWIFE

USA TODAY Bestselling Author

CASSIE MILES

To Christine Jorgensen and the Monday Think Tank.
And, as always, to Rick.

Recycling programs for this product may not exist in your area.

ISBN-13: 978-0-373-74689-7

MOMMY MIDWIFE

This edition published by arrangement with Harlequin Books S.A.

For questions and comments about the quality of this book please contact us at Customer_eCare@Harlequin.ca.

www.Harlequin.com

Printed in U.S.A.

ABOUT THE AUTHOR

Though born in Chicago and raised in L.A., *USA TODAY* bestselling author Cassie Miles has lived in Colorado long enough to be considered a semi-native. The first home she owned was a log cabin in the mountains overlooking Elk Creek, with a thirty-mile commute to her work at the *Denver Post*.

After raising two daughters and cooking tons of macaroni and cheese for her family, Cassie is trying to be more adventurous in her culinary efforts. Ceviche, anyone? She's discovered that almost anything tastes better with wine. When she's not plotting Harlequin Intrigue books, Cassie likes to hang out at the Denver Botanical Gardens near her high-rise home.

Books by Cassie Miles

HARLEQUIN INTRIGUE

904—UNDERCOVER COLORADO**
910—MURDER ON THE MOUNTAIN**
948—FOOTPRINTS IN THE SNOW
978—PROTECTIVE CONFINEMENT*
984—COMPROMISED SECURITY*
999—NAVAJO ECHOES
1025—CHRISTMAS COVER-UP
1048—MYSTERIOUS MILLIONAIRE
1074—IN THE MANOR WITH THE MILLIONAIRE
1102—CHRISTMAS CRIME IN COLORADO
1126—CRIMINALLY HANDSOME
1165—COLORADO ABDUCTION‡
1171—BODYGUARD UNDER THE MISTLETOE‡
1177—SECLUDED WITH THE COWBOY‡
1193—INDESTRUCTIBLE
1223—LOCK, STOCK AND SECRET BABY‡‡
1229—HOOK, LINE AND SHOTGUN BRIDE‡‡
1255—MOUNTAIN MIDWIFE
1279—UNFORGETTABLE
1293—SOVEREIGN SHERIFF
1317—BABY BATTALION
1343—MIDWIFE COVER
1368—MOMMY MIDWIFE

**Rocky Mountain Safe House
*Safe House: Mesa Verde
‡Christmas at the Carlisles'
‡‡Special Delivery Babies

CAST OF CHARACTERS

Olivia Laughton—Eight and a half months pregnant, the midwife is about to become a mommy.

Troy Weathers—The baby's father wants to marry Olivia but isn't ready to give up his career as a marine captain in special ops.

Alex Weathers—Troy's brother is a doctor who works in the E.R. and at a homeless clinic.

Bianca Laughton—Olivia's sister, a lawyer, is on her way toward partnership in her firm.

Richard and Sharon Laughton—Olivia's diplomat parents have kept their life-changing secret for years.

Sergeant Blaine Nelson—Troy's second-in-command is running the show on the investigation into a terrorist cell code named Hatari.

Kruger—A legendary undercover operative who entered the U.S. more than twenty years ago has linked with the Hatari terrorists.

Prince Amir—The powerful Saudi prince is attracted to Bianca.

Matthew Clark—A top executive in an oil company, he is a client of Bianca's law firm and a man with many secrets.

Jarvis Raines—A former client of Olivia's, he blames her for the death of his baby.

Carol Raines—The trauma of losing her baby propelled her to help others at the homeless clinic run by Alex.

Prologue

Cold and alone, Olivia Laughton shuffled aimlessly through the dark streets of Denver. A stiff November wind rattled the last of the dead, dry leaves clinging to the branches, and she clutched the broken zipper on the front of her borrowed sweatshirt, a navy blue rag she'd discovered in the hospital lost and found office. She'd left her bloodstained parka behind.

She couldn't throw away her memories so easily. In horrible detail, she recalled the scene of the car accident in the mountains, the chopper that brought her and the victims into town and the E.R. staff who told her there was nothing more she could do for them. *There was always something more.* She was a nurse. She should have tried one more procedure. She should have found a way to save them.

A sob crawled up her throat but she was too numb to make a sound. All she could do was keep walking, step after step, mile after mile. If she stood still, the gathering sorrow would rise up and roll over her like an avalanche. Would she still feel pain when she was frozen in a solid block of ice?

Though she hadn't planned her destination, her surroundings were familiar. Stumbling to a halt, she looked to her right and saw the beige brick bungalow where Alex Weathers lived. Alex was a doctor; he'd hold her hand and tell her that everything was okay. *It's not your fault.* That was what he'd say. And she wouldn't believe him.

Seeing Alex wouldn't help her. His brother, Troy, was a different story. When she thought of him, she felt a burst of heat in her belly. Troy Weathers would give her what she needed. He'd take her in his arms and make her forget what happened. With Troy, she could purge her memory.

Did she dare approach him? They'd been on only two dates. Once for coffee. Once for lunch. There had been a fiery kiss that left her craving more, and he'd promised that he'd call her the next time he was in Denver. In spite of their nearly combustible chemistry, she didn't make the mistake of thinking they were headed toward a relationship. They had nothing in common. She was a nurse midwife, a healer. And he was a career marine in special ops, a dangerous man.

Unaware of moving toward the porch light,

she found herself standing at the front door. She pressed the buzzer.

Troy opened the door. "Olivia?"

Through the screen door, she stared into his dark brown eyes. "I need you."

He pulled her inside. The light from a table lamp glared in her eyes, and she blinked until the room came into focus—a typical bachelor pad with mismatched furniture. The lamplight shone on the spine of an open book. Odd. She never would have thought a man of action like Troy would spend his spare time reading.

"Alex isn't here," he said. "He's working a night shift."

"I don't want Alex."

The warmth inside the house penetrated the cold that wrapped around her like a shroud. Her skin prickled as her heart began to pump and her blood began to flow.

"You look like hell," he said.

She couldn't say the same about him. He looked damn good. With his wide shoulders and narrow hips, he made the black Mickey Mouse T-shirt he wore seem sexy. Even in his bare feet, he towered over her. His sinewy, tanned forearms were cut to perfection. She wanted his arms around her, wanted to feel him inside her.

Was she really doing this? Showing up on the doorstep of a casual acquaintance and demanding sex? Never before had she done anything so desperate. She was the type of person who took care of others, not the other way around. She prided herself on being able to handle any crisis. Not this time. Never before had she felt so shattered.

Her arms fell loosely to her sides, and the oversize sweatshirt gaped open. Troy stared at her T-shirt.

"That's blood," he said.

"Yes."

"Are you injured?"

"It's not mine."

"Do I need to call 911?"

She was puzzled. "Why?"

"Well, if it's not your blood, there's somebody else out there who's in need of first aid."

"You think I killed someone?"

"Did you?"

If she could have mustered the energy, she would have laughed at the absurdity of his suggestion. "No."

"What happened?"

He deserved an explanation, and she wanted to give him one. But she couldn't force herself to tell him. She gasped. Her lungs ached, and her throat was raw. The sobs she'd been holding back threatened to gush from her. She shook her head, and her vision blurred. She felt herself beginning to hyperventilate.

"Hey," he said. "Pull it together, woman."

His voice was like a slap in the face. "What?"

"You heard me. If there's one thing I can't stand, it's to see a woman cry."

"Don't worry." With an effort, she stiffened her spine. "I'm not going to have a breakdown."

"Good." He took her hand. His gentle touch contrasted the authority in his voice. "You're freezing. Come with me."

She followed him down the hallway, glad to let him take control. In the bathroom, he flicked on the overhead light. The clear shower curtain was decorated with a map of the world, and the countertop was littered with shaving supplies, which Troy hadn't been using lately. His square jaw was covered with stubble, a rugged contrast to his neat-trimmed black hair.

"You've got blood all over," he said. "It's on your shirt and your jeans. Even in your hair."

She glanced into the mirror. A brownish smear matted in the tangles of long blond hair that had escaped her ponytail. Quickly, she looked away. "I'm a mess."

"I've seen worse," he said. "Now, here's what's going to happen. First, you need to get cleaned up. You're going to strip and take a shower. Okay? And I'll bring you something to wear."

She stumbled toward the toilet, flipped down the seat and sat. The prospect of washing up felt like a monumental undertaking. She stared at the shower curtain map, wishing she were somewhere else, somewhere far away. Was coming here a mistake?

"Come on, Olivia. You've got to get out of those clothes."

"I know."

"Just relax. Talk to me." He knelt on the tile floor in front of her and untied the laces on her sneakers. "Tell me what you're doing in Denver. You live up in the mountains, right?"

"In Dillon." She had a private practice as a midwife and also worked at the hospitals in Summit County, but she came to Denver twice a month to assist at a clinic for the homeless. That was where she'd met Alex.

"What are you doing in town?" he repeated as he pulled off her right shoe and sock. "You can tell me anything. Where did the blood come from? Was there an accident?"

"Car accident. Then the helicopter came." She remembered the roar of the rotors, shouts from the crew, the endless scream. "It was loud."

"Yeah, choppers are like that." He took off her other shoe and sock. "You went to the hospital."

She nodded. "E.R."

"And then what?"

A mental door slammed shut. "I can't. I don't want to talk about it."

His large hand rested on her knee, and he gazed into her eyes. “You might find this hard to believe, but I know where you’re coming from.”

Anger whipped through her. “How can you possibly know?”

“I can see that you’ve been through something bad, really bad.” He stood and hovered over her. “Do you need help with that sweatshirt?”

She growled, “I can undress myself.”

“There’s nothing wrong with asking for help, you know.”

“A nice little chat,” she said bitterly. It would take more than that to heal her.

“It’s a place to start. After you take your shower and get cleaned up, I’ll make you something warm to drink.”

“If I’d wanted tea and sensitivity, I would have come looking for your brother.”

“Fair enough,” Troy said. “What do you want from me?”

She surged to her feet. Reaching up, she held his face with both hands and kissed him. His mouth was hard as stone, but that didn’t stop her. Her tongue traced the line of his lips and she kissed him again.

Though he held back, she wrapped her arms around his neck and pressed her body against him. “Make love to me, Troy.”

He tried to push her away, but she clung tighter.

He tried to reason with her, but she wouldn't listen.

Desperation consumed her. She needed to feel life pulsing inside her. She needed the heat of passion to melt the icy fingers that held her heart in a frozen grip.

Another kiss. Another frantic caress. She could feel him beginning to respond. "Please," she begged. "Please."

His arms embraced her. His mouth found hers, and he breathed new life into her lungs.

Tonight, they would make love.

After that, she never expected to see him again.

Chapter One

Eight and a half months later...

Today was a first for Olivia. Triplets, she'd delivered triplets! She rubbed her hand over the swell of her own hugely pregnant belly, glad that there was only one bun in this oven. Three were way too many to handle as a single mom. Her one baby—a boy—was the perfect number, just perfect. Nearly every aspect of her pregnancy was perfect.

After a last peek at the three healthy baby girls in the hospital nursery, she headed down the corridor toward the front exit of St. Agnes Hospital in Summit County. Tired but happy, she stepped outside and inhaled a breath of fresh mountain air.

The last glow of sunset was fading from the August skies, leaving a faint gold outline along the hogback ridge opposite the hospital complex. The summer night was quiet and warm enough that she didn't really need the cardigan she'd thrown on over her purple scrubs. She set her backpack on the pavement beside a stone bench, stretched her arms over her head and yawned.

It had been a twelve-hour labor with many anxious moments. At one point, Olivia had considered calling for a C-section, but the mom had insisted that she'd get a second wind. And she'd been correct. When the time had come to push, the babies had arrived without complications, other than the juggling act required to handle three newborns at the same time.

Before crossing the parking lot to her SUV, Olivia sat on the bench to check the phone messages that had accumulated on her cell. The first had come at sixteen minutes past four o'clock.

"Hey, pretty lady." It was Troy. "I'm in Denver, and I want to get together. Call me back."

Eight and a half months ago, she'd needed him desperately. Now…not so much. She patted her belly and deleted his message.

Erasing the man himself wasn't so easy. The next phone message at precisely five o'clock was also from him. "Don't think you'll get rid of me by not calling back. If necessary, I'll use military intelligence resources to triangulate your phone signal, pinpoint your exact location and find you."

"Like a stalker," she muttered as she pressed Delete.

His third message came only fifteen minutes after the second. And it was brief. "Marry me, Olivia."

"No way," she said to the phone. What did it take to get through to this man? This had to be the twentieth time that he'd proposed.

When she was four months pregnant, he'd been back in Denver, and she'd told him the news. He had the right to know that he'd fathered a child and that it was her intention to keep the baby and raise it on her own. At age thirty, her biological clock had been clanging like a fire siren. She wanted this baby with all her heart, and she'd made it crystal clear to Troy that she would not require child support and would allow him all the visitation rights he wanted.

His response had been to drop to one knee and propose. She should have known he'd take responsibility. The man was a career marine, and he was all about honor and duty.

Short-sighted was what she called that attitude. Her grandma always said, "Marry in haste and regret it at leisure." Olivia had thanked Troy for being considerate, but she'd told him no, absolutely not, no.

Her refusal didn't stop him from proposing again. And again. And again. Every time she saw him or heard from him, he popped the question. He'd sent a dozen roses on her birthday—a date she hadn't told him but he'd somehow figured out. In the flowers was a card that said, Marry me, Olivia.

Then he'd started sending baby gifts. A tiny Yankees baseball cap, a hand-crocheted blanket, a teddy bear and a three-wheel jogging stroller that was perfect for the mountains. If they'd been in love, she would have been touched. But they weren't.

She hit the delete button.

The last message from Troy said, "I'm guessing that you're busy, probably delivering somebody else's baby. See you soon."

That sounded like he was giving up. Though she should have been glad to avoid another awkward encounter, she felt a twinge of disappointment. Even if she wasn't going to marry the man, she had to admit that his attention made her feel special.

The final message on her cell was from her mother. "Your father and I just arrived at your sister's house in Denver, and we're exhausted. The flight from Cairo took forever, and then we had a four-hour briefing in D.C., which was dreadfully boring. We're very much looking forward to seeing you tomorrow. Call in the morning, dear."

Olivia groaned. Her globe-hopping diplomat parents had probably rearranged the schedules of kings, sheiks and ambassadors to be here for the birth of their first grandchild. This was a grand event, and they had certain expectations, ranging from the name of the baby to their insistence that she check into a hospital to give birth—a demand that was totally insulting. Olivia was a midwife, after all. An expert when it came to delivering babies. Hadn't she just handled the birth of triplets? Still, her mom claimed to know better.

She tucked her phone into her oversize purse and rose from the bench. As she stepped off the curb, she caught a glimpse of movement from the corner of her eye. And she heard a sound—a mechanical, clicking noise. A gun being cocked?

Startled, she turned her head and peered into the scraggly stand of pine trees beyond the parking lot lights. No one was there. The lot was deserted. Listening hard, she told herself that she'd imagined the noise. It was only the snap of a twig, nothing to be afraid of.

A group of nurses emerged from the front door of the hospital complex. One of them waved to her and shouted congratulations on the triplets. She waved back as she hurried across the pavement and dived behind the wheel of her SUV.

She locked the doors and sat for a moment, catching her breath. Though she hadn't actually seen anyone, she still had the sense of being watched. This wasn't the first time. For the past several days, she'd been on edge. Was paranoia a side effect of raging hormones?

After a struggle with the seat belt, she started her SUV and drove out of the lot. Maybe she was nervous because she felt vulnerable in her pregnant body. If attacked, how would she defend herself? She couldn't break into a sprint. Nor could she throw a karate chop. A high-flying kick was out of the question. The only way she could fight back was to sit on her attacker and crush him to death with her massive belly.

The headlights of her SUV cut through the thick forest on the way to her house. *Nobody is after me.* Why would they be? She wasn't a woman of mystery. Her life was an open book—a fairly dull book, the kind you read to put yourself to sleep. *Nothing terrible is going to happen.* Her overactive imagination was simply a reflection of her fears about having this baby. Unnecessary fears. She had everything under control.

The couple with the triplets had been the last clients she intended to see for a while. She'd arranged with another midwife to handle her practice for the next three months. After that, Olivia would ease back into a regular schedule. Handling a newborn and working wouldn't be easy, but she was better prepared than most new mothers and had great connections for child care.

She'd almost talked herself into a state of calm

when she pulled into the wide gravel driveway outside her detached garage. On the other side of her withered attempt at an herb garden was her two-bedroom, ranch-style cabin. Before she turned off the engine, she noticed that the light in her bedroom was on. Had she forgotten to turn it off this morning? It didn't seem likely. When she'd left the house this morning, it was already daylight. Had she remembered to lock the doors? Was somebody inside, waiting for her?

Her fingers tensed on the steering wheel as she considered driving away and getting help. She'd look like a fool if there was nothing wrong, but it was better to be ridiculous than to take risks.

A black SUV drove up beside her and parked. She didn't recognize the vehicle. Her first impulse was to throw her car into Reverse and zoom away, but she didn't have time. The instant the SUV parked, a man got out—a tall man with neat-trimmed black hair and a square jaw. It was Troy.

He strolled up to her driver's side window, and she lowered it. She was glad to see him. If there was an intruder in her house, she could do worse than having a marine to defend her.

"The light in my bedroom window," she said. "I'm sure I didn't leave it on this morning."

"Stay in the car." His easygoing grin disappeared. "If there's trouble, I want you to drive away fast. Call 911."

She didn't like being chased away from her own house, but she nodded. "What are you going to do?"

"Take care of the situation."

"Wait." She detached the house key from her key chain and handed it to him. "You need this to get inside."

"Not really."

"Please don't kick my door down."

He pocketed the key, pushed aside his tan windbreaker and drew an automatic weapon from a belt holster. His approach to the house was quick and stealthy, keeping to the shadows. Why was he carrying a gun?

APPROACHING THE CABIN, Troy forgot about pleading his case for marriage to Olivia and went into warrior mode. After fourteen years in special ops and military intelligence, he was always on high alert. The world was full of threats. His job was to neutralize the danger.

First, he needed to clear the perimeter around her house. Being careful not to walk in front of windows and present himself as a target, he held his weapon at the ready as he circled the rectangular log cabin with the shake shingle roof.

He'd been to this house only once before, and that was a brief visit. He knew that Olivia had zero security. Any of the windows could be easily opened, and the door locks could be picked by a third-grader with a paper clip.

When he was satisfied that no one was lurking outside the house, he prepared to enter. This was the tricky part. If the intruders waited inside for an ambush, they'd have weapons trained on the door. Troy would have preferred going through a window but the casements were chest-high and climbing through would require both hands. Remembering her wish that he not destroy her property, he used the key, shoved the front door open and stepped back, using the solid log wall as a shield.

No gunfire. No sound from within. He rushed the entrance and went through the house, room by room, closet by closet, turning on lights as he went. The house was all clear. As far as he could tell, she hadn't been robbed.

On his prior visit, he hadn't made it as far as the bedroom, and he took a moment to look around. The furniture was traditional but not plain—a reflection of Olivia, who was a mix of sweet homespun and aggressive independence. He ran his fingertips across the front of a wardrobe that was painted with vines and purple columbines. The lamp on her bedside table had shiny crystals dangling from the shade.

If intruders had turned that lamp on, they would have been here after dark. Not that long ago. He hoped there hadn't been a break-in. More likely, this was a simple case of Olivia leaving the light on and forgetting that she'd done so. Still, he knew better than to dismiss a threat without thoroughly checking it out.

The second bedroom was painted a soft blue, not unlike the color of her eyes. It was the nursery, the room where his baby boy would sleep. Would their son have her eyes? Troy swallowed the lump in his throat that came whenever he thought of the baby. Never in his life had he been the least bit sentimental, and he'd given considerable thought to why he was touched by the idea of having a family.

His age had something to do with these feelings. On his last birthday, Troy turned thirty-six. In most professions, he'd still be considered young, but that wasn't true for special ops. His vision wasn't as sharp as it should be for a sniper. His reflexes had slowed by a few milliseconds, enough that it made a difference. He wasn't at his physical peak, and he realized that it was time for him to step back and take a more supervisory role. Becoming a father and having a family seemed like the natural next step in his life.

He liked the simple, clean furnishings in the nursery: a dark oak crib, matching changing table and rocking chair. Seated in the rocker was the teddy bear he'd sent—fuzzy and brown and dressed in camo fatigues. He wanted to see his son holding the bear, wanted to show him how to play catch and to take him fishing. He wanted to be a real part of his child's life. Somehow, he had to convince Olivia.

He returned to her SUV where she had prudently stayed behind the steering wheel with the doors locked. With wide eyes, she peered through the driver's side window.

"There's nobody inside," he said. He looked to the next obvious hiding place for an intruder. "Do you usually park in the garage?"

"Not when the weather is nice."

"Leave your headlights on and hit the automatic door opener."

Holding his weapon at the ready, he moved to the side of the square structure. The garage door squawked and rumbled as it folded up on itself. The interior held the typical junk that accumulates in a garage as well as ski equipment and a very nice mountain bike with heavy-duty tires.

Troy noticed the outline of a footprint in the dust on the concrete floor. It appeared to be a man-size boot, too large for Olivia. The print could have been made today or last week or a month ago. He checked the side door to the garage. It was open.

"Olivia," he called to her. "Is this door usually locked?"

"It should be," she yelled back to him. "But I usually don't bother."

None of the boxes or tools in the garage looked like they'd been disturbed. If an intruder had searched in here, he'd been incredibly careful. And why bother being so stealthy in a garage? It didn't make sense.

Troy decided against mentioning the footprint. Not right now, anyway. He returned to her SUV. "I think we're okay."

"Are you sure? Could you tell if anything was stolen?"

"It doesn't look like it." Her nervousness seemed out of proportion for a light left on in a window, and it wasn't like her to panic for no reason. "What's going on? Have you been threatened before this?"

"Why would I be threatened? I'm just a midwife."

As she pushed open her car door and climbed out, his gaze focused on her belly. He hadn't seen her for two months, and she'd swelled up like a watermelon. His fingers itched to touch her roundness. "You look beautiful."

"Yeah, right." She lurched past him toward the cabin. "I'm gorgeous if you're into pre-Columbian fertility goddesses."

He followed in her wake, watching the sway

of her hips under her purple scrubs. Pregnant women didn't usually excite him, but he had an overpowering urge to caress her and hold her miraculous body against his.

Inside the cabin, she dropped her satchel-size purse on the green plaid sofa and peeled off her light sweater. Her breasts were full and ripe. Troy suppressed a growl. "How are you feeling?"

"I'll ask the questions," she said as she turned to the left and strode into the kitchen. Striding didn't exactly describe the way she moved. She rolled a bit from side to side as though she were walking on the deck of a ship.

She turned on the water and reached for a glass from the cabinet to the right of the sink. "First question. How did you know where to find me?"

"Wasn't hard. I called the hospital where you usually work and found out you were there. When I pulled into the parking lot and didn't see your car, I came here." He paused. "The nurse told me that you were with a mom who was having triplets. How did that work out?"

"Amazing. That word is overused. People say everything is amazing, but this really was. Truly a miracle." Her grin was pure happiness. "Next question. What are you doing here?"

He was sick and tired of popping the question that was always answered with an emphatic no. "I wanted to see you."

"Why?"

"Since we're playing a question game," he said, "I have one for you. One I've never asked before."

She took another sip of water and eyed him suspiciously. "All right. Shoot."

"When you found out you were pregnant, what made you decide to keep the baby?"

"Dumb question," she said. "I love babies and always planned to have a family. Plus, I'm thirty, which is a good age for a healthy pregnancy. And you played a part in my decision."

"Did I?"

"Of course," she said as though it was the most obvious thing in the world. "I mean, look at you. You're physically healthy and fairly intelligent. I'd have to say that you're an excellent candidate to be a sperm donor."

"Gee, thanks."

She crossed the kitchen to the refrigerator and reached for the handle. Her hand dropped to her side. Frozen, she stared at the white refrigerator door where dozens of photographs were attached with magnets.

"What's wrong?" he asked.

"There was a photo of me, my sister and our parents on a vacation we took last year. It's missing."

"Are you certain?"

She pointed to a vacant space on the refrigerator door. “It was right here. And it’s gone. Someone was in my cabin.”

Chapter Two

After Troy got down on his hands and knees to check around the edges of the cabinets and the floor where a photo might have fallen, he was ready to believe her. An intruder or intruders had entered her cabin and stolen a picture from the fridge. Why bother? A straightforward burglary would have made more sense.

"I want you to look around," he said. "See if anything else was taken, maybe jewelry or documents."

"I don't have any valuable jewelry."

"A family photo doesn't have any intrinsic value, either. Just take a look."

He followed her as she quickly rifled through a small jewelry box in her bedroom. In the living room, she sat at her desk and started sorting through the file drawers.

His thoughts focused on risk assessment. On intelligence missions, he was accustomed to walking into a situation and determining the course of action. He needed to know why her house had been broken into. If he figured out what the bad guys wanted, he'd know how far they'd go to get it.

"Was there anything unusual in that photo?" he asked.

"Not really. We were standing in the backyard at my sister's house in Denver."

"Who took the picture?"

"My sister's boyfriend."

"Tell me about the background. And the clothing."

Olivia squinted as she remembered. "It was at a family barbecue last summer. There was a blue spruce behind us. We were all dressed casual. My dad had on a god-awful pair of plaid shorts. He's tall and has really skinny legs. Like a stork."

He nodded. Actually, he'd learned a great deal about her parents. The life history of Richard and Sharon Laughton made for interesting reading, especially for someone like Troy who had a high security clearance. "Can you think of any reason someone would steal this particular picture?"

"It was just us. The Laughton family at play."

The obvious answer was that the photo would be used for identification. Though pregnancy had vastly altered her appearance, she still resembled the woman in the photo.

Troy had only one other clue: the footprint in

the garage. Why would the intruder have gone into her garage other than to search? A lightbulb went on in his head. The bad guys were hiding in the garage, setting an ambush. "I know what's going on."

"Oh, good." She swiveled in the chair behind her desk and looked up at him. "Because I can't find anything missing in my documents. Most of my confidential stuff is on my laptop computer, and I took that with me to the hospital."

"The intruder or intruders were in your garage, waiting for you to come home."

Her hand fluttered to her mouth, covering a frightened gasp. "Do you think they were there when I pulled up?"

"It's possible." Troy cursed himself for not searching the garage first. He could have ended this before it escalated.

"Why? What do they want?"

"Nothing is missing. So I'm guessing that their intention wasn't robbery."

"Then what?"

"They wanted to take…you."

She looked away from him, shielding her gaze as though she had something to hide. "A kidnap attempt."

"You don't seem too surprised."

"I've had a feeling for the past couple of days." Her hands rested protectively on her belly. "It's been like someone is watching me. Earlier tonight in the hospital parking lot, I thought I heard a gun being cocked."

The situation was more intense than he thought. They needed to retreat to a safe location. "You have five minutes to get packed."

"Kidnapping doesn't make any sense."

"Later, we'll talk. Now, get packed."

"No. I'm not going to leave my house until I understand."

He braced his hands on the arms of her chair and leaned close. Being near her was a distraction, for sure. The blue of her eyes contrasted her healthy tan and the pink flush of her cheeks. Was she glowing? Later, he'd take the time to appreciate the miraculous changes in her body. Right now, he needed for her to cooperate.

"The standard reasons for kidnapping," he said, "are money or leverage. The intruders want to use you and our baby to get something they want."

"It can't be for ransom money. My family isn't superrich."

"Your mom and dad are in Denver this weekend."

"How do you know that?" she demanded.

"I'm in intelligence," he reminded her. "They're in town, right?"

"Staying with my sister, Bianca. They want me to move in with her until after the baby is born."

"They want to protect you," he said.

"From what?"

He held her chin, forcing her to look directly at him. "I know about your parents."

She blinked, an automatic response from someone who had spent her entire life living with lies. "I have no idea what you're talking about."

"Richard and Sharon Laughton work for the CIA. They're spies."

THOUGH IT WAS still hard to believe that she was the target of a kidnapping plot, Olivia couldn't take chances in her present condition. She had to leave her cabin.

In the bedroom, she threw some of her belongings into a suitcase. Most of her pregnancy clothes didn't fit anymore, making packing easy. She took everything she could still wear, even the fancy, lavender crepe toga-style gown that she'd bought for a hospital fundraiser.

Troy stood watch, slouching against the doorjamb with his gun in hand. Though his posture was relaxed, she could see the tension coiling through him. At the slightest provocation, he was ready to strike. This was a side of him that she hadn't seen before—a little bit scary but also reassuring. If he hadn't shown up at her house when he did, she could have been in real trouble.

"You know," she said, "my parents aren't the

kind of spies who do what you do. They don't go on active missions."

"Sure." Somehow, he made that one terse word sound like he didn't believe her.

"They work in embassies. My dad is a paper-pusher, and my mother is a cultural attaché. She hangs out with ballet dancers and artists. She arranges events."

"Are you done packing?"

She'd already scooped all her bathroom toiletries and hair stuff into a plastic bag that was at the bottom of the suitcase. Tossing in a book from the nightstand, she gave him a nod. "That's everything."

"We're taking my car," he said.

She objected. "There's nothing wrong with my car, and I'm going to need it when we're in Denver."

"If it becomes necessary to use evasive driving techniques, you'll be glad I wrecked the rental instead of your car."

A shudder went through her. "I hope that's a joke."

"I'm not laughing." His eyebrows pinched in a scowl that made his dark eyes even more fierce and intense. "From now on, we do things my way. This is my job, Olivia. I know how to keep you safe. Don't argue with me every step of the way."

His macho take-charge attitude would have been

irritating if the potential for danger hadn't been so real. She reminded herself that there had been intruders in her garage, waiting to grab her. For a while, her independent nature was going to have to take a backseat. "I understand."

"We'll turn out all the lights," he said. "I'll go first. You follow with the suitcase. Take it around to the back of the SUV, and then get in the passenger side. Move as quickly as possible."

"That's not real fast."

"If I tell you to get down, hit the dirt."

She really hoped that maneuver wouldn't be necessary. In spite of her pilates and yoga exercises, she was just about as graceful as a hippo when she had to get up and down off the floor.

After he'd turned off the lights, they stood inside by the front door for a moment, allowing their eyes to adjust to the dark. Troy moved to the edge of her front window and peered into the front yard.

She asked, "Do you see anything?"

"Visibility isn't great. I could really use a pair of infrared goggles." He gave her arm a reassuring squeeze. "There's no telling what we'll find around the corner of the garage. But you don't need to worry. I'll be in front. Ready?"

"I guess."

He eased open the door. Immediately, they

were moving through her moonlit yard. She followed him, pulling her suitcase, struggling to keep up as he rushed forward.

Her pulse thumped hard. Adrenaline raced through her system. At the driveway, she dragged the suitcase to the back of his SUV, went to the passenger seat and climbed in. Before she'd finished struggling with the seat belt, he had loaded her suitcase and was in the driver's seat. He started the engine, whipped into Reverse and zipped away from her cabin.

A glance at the speedometer showed her that he was well over the recommended speed limit for this narrow, winding road, but she wasn't scared. Troy had control of the vehicle. He was fast but safe.

She craned her neck to look over her shoulder. She didn't see headlights behind them. "Are we safe?"

"I don't see anyone."

The narrow road straightened a bit as they drove past a beaver pond. It was less than a mile to a main intersection. "What happens if they catch up to us?"

"They won't." He negotiated the rugged road like a grand prix champion. "I think we made our escape fast enough that they didn't have time to plan another assault. It's a good thing that you noticed that missing photo."

"And a really good thing that you were with me."

He cranked the steering wheel, and the SUV swerved onto a paved road. There was no other traffic in sight.

Breathing hard, she flopped back against the seat. This definitely wasn't the evening she'd expected after a long day at the hospital. In usual circumstances, she would have thrown together a salad with fresh veggies, had a cup of tea and relaxed. No doubt, her poor feet were swollen. Her sneakers felt as tight as rubber bands.

Absentmindedly, she stroked her tight belly. Inside her, the baby started to kick, possibly in reaction to the rush of adrenaline when she fled the cabin. "Wow, it feels like he's jumping hurdles."

"Who's doing what?"

"The baby. He's bouncing around."

Troy kept his eyes on the road, but reached his hand toward her. "May I?"

She appreciated that he asked. So many people walked right up to her and began touching without permission. Gently, she took his hand and placed it over the place where the child—their child—was tap dancing.

Troy reacted, pulling his hand away. "That's the baby?"

"Oh, yeah. I think he got excited by our escape. I don't do a lot of running these days."

"It doesn't hurt him, does it? I mean, he's okay, right?"

His concern erased his macho facade. Feeling the baby move had turned this big, bad marine into a cream puff. His reaction was actually kind of cute.

"The baby's fine," she assured him. "He's always active. Sometimes, I think he's got a ping-pong paddle in there."

Troy replaced his hand on her belly. As he experienced more kicks, a wide grin spread across his face. "That's my boy."

She shared his pride. After all the time and effort she'd spent resisting Troy, she felt closer to him now than ever before. Strange. When they'd made love the first time, it had been because of a personal disaster. Now, it took another potential disaster to bring them together.

"Where are we going?" she asked.

"We could continue on into Denver or stop at a hotel on the way. Your choice."

"Hotel," she said. "I'm too tired to face my parents tonight."

"Lucky for us, I already have a suite booked in Keystone."

"Why would you make reservations?"

"I needed a place to stay after you threw me out. Again."

Was she really that mean? The answer, of course, was yes. She'd been pushing him away with both hands for eight and a half months, but she wasn't going to apologize. She had her reasons. "Does this hotel have room service?"

"Count on it." He gave her tummy a final pat and took his hand away. "Tonight, I'll pamper you. This is a nice place, and you can have anything you want to eat."

"Yay, I almost feel good about having my house broken into."

"As soon as we get there, you need to call your parents and tell them what happened. The photo on the fridge was of all four of you. They might also be targets."

She knew his analysis of the situation was correct. If someone was after her, the rest of her family could be in danger. Telling them would be difficult, nearly impossible. "Their work isn't something we talk about. Not ever."

When she and her sister were growing up, they knew their parents had contacts that went beyond their jobs in the diplomatic corps, and they had learned not to ask too many questions when their parents left town.

"Did your family travel a lot?" he asked.

"When I was little we did. But we were based

in Washington, D.C., for years and years. I'd have to say that I had a very average childhood."

Aware that she was swimming in a sea of denial, Olivia turned her head and stared through the window at the thick pine forest beside the road. No matter how many times she told herself that her early life was as normal as puppy dogs and lollipops, it was a lie.

"You can tell me the truth," he said.

"What do you mean?"

"I have a high security clearance, and I've looked into your background thoroughly."

"I don't like that. I have a right to my privacy."

For a few moments, he drove in silence. Then he cleared his throat and spoke again. "When you were a child, you and your mother were abducted and held captive for a week."

He had flung open a door to her past that she always kept tightly locked. This was her secret, her life. And she didn't want to look back.

Chapter Three

Troy knew that he'd overstepped his boundaries with Olivia, but he wasn't going to let the subject drop. Not when her safety had been compromised. She needed to understand that her parents' profession might be the reason she was targeted for kidnapping. It wasn't the first time she'd been abducted.

"Stop the car," she said. "I want out."

"That's not going to happen. I won't let you put yourself and our child in danger."

"There's nobody following us. You said so yourself."

"You need a bodyguard, and I'm here. Deal with it."

Months ago, when he'd first started researching her past, he'd felt bad about poking around where he hadn't been invited, but he'd rationalized it by telling himself that it was his right to know everything he could about the mother of his child. Since she'd made it clear that she didn't want to talk to him, what choice did he have? But he'd gone deeper than he'd originally intended when he'd discovered that she was the daughter of two international spies. He never would have guessed that she had such an exotic background.

His first impression of Olivia had been that she was a practical, down-to-earth woman—a healthy, easygoing mountain gal who didn't wear makeup and liked being outdoors. When she'd showed up on his brother's doorstep and demanded sex, he'd revised that opinion to include passionate. That night, she'd made love like there was no tomorrow. He'd never forget the way she rode him with her blond hair flying in wild tangles and her slender body arched above him. Her small, firm breasts had glistened in the light from a bedside lamp. She'd driven him to a height he'd never reached before. It was no wonder that he hadn't noticed when the condom had slipped.

After that night, he'd wanted to spend more time with her, but she'd shut him down. He'd returned to his assignment in the Middle East and had tried to forget her. Olivia Laughton would be the one who got away—the woman he'd see only in his fantasies.

Her announcement that she was carrying his child changed his plans, and that was when he'd started digging. Her parents intrigued him. By all accounts, they were charming and sophisticated diplomats. To uncover their connection to the CIA, Troy called in favors from high-ranking sources in the intelligence community. He didn't know specifics about their assignments, but he had learned of an incident in a South American country that changed the careers of Richard and Sharon Laughton. That incident involved their seven-year-old daughter.

He glanced over at her. "I can't force you to talk to me, but it's important for us to figure out who's after you. Anything you can remember might be helpful."

"You're right," she admitted in a small voice. "I hate that you're right, but you are."

"You can tell me anything. I won't be shocked."

She exhaled a heavy sigh. "Do you think there's a connection between the kidnapping when I was a child and what's happening now?"

"I don't know."

She turned away from him with her face in shadow. If he could have seen her expression, he'd have had a better idea of what was going on in her head. Either she would decide to trust him with her secrets or she'd keep that door closed. He hoped for the former.

"It wasn't that bad," she said. "When you think of being held captive, it seems like a horror story. But it wasn't."

He said nothing, not wanting to interrupt her

fragile narrative. There were more vehicles on the road to Keystone, both coming and going. He kept careful watch in the rearview mirror to make sure they weren't being tailed.

"Our family was stationed in a South American country," she said. "I don't even remember which one. I was only seven, and life was kind of a blur, living in one place after another. My sister was four and she was with the nanny all the time. I had more freedom. Our residence was a square with a patio and garden in the middle, which was where I spent most of my time. We had servants, and I played with their kids. Though I wasn't aware of learning the language, I spoke Spanish as often as English."

As she continued, her voice became more sure and steady. They were only a few minutes away from their destination, and he decided to prolong their trip so she'd keep talking. He cranked the steering wheel, and the rented SUV made a sharp left.

"Where are we going?" she asked. "This isn't the way to Keystone."

"I'm doubling back to make sure we aren't being followed."

Her slender hand rested atop her belly. "You know, I've never talked about this before. It doesn't even seem like it happened to me. The memory is more like a movie I saw or something I read in a book."

Hoping to get her back to the story, he prompted, "Did you have your own room at the residence?"

"I sure did. And a canopy bed with a pink duvet and lots of flounces. The room where my parents slept was huge with a giant walk-in closet. I loved to watch my mother getting all dressed up for special events. The night when the incident took place, she wore a dark blue V-neck dress with long sleeves and shoulder pads. Remember shoulder pads? My mom always wore them. It was that power dressing thing."

She was loosening up, and he encouraged her. "I've seen photos of your mother. She's an attractive woman."

"Beautiful and classy. My sister looks a lot like her. Me? Not really. We all have blond hair, that's about it."

He thought Olivia was beautiful, and he'd told her a million times. But that wasn't the point right now. "When you were a child, did you know what your parents did?"

"They worked at the embassy. That's all I knew. That's typical, isn't it? Most kids don't have a clue what their parents actually do for a living."

"Most kids don't have spies for parents."

"And they don't get abducted," she said. "Okay, now I've started this story, I want to get through it."

"I'm listening."

"My mom was all dressed up. Since my dad was already at the party, I went to the front of the house with her to wait for the limo that would take her to the party. A big, shiny car pulled up. A strange man got out and talked to her in a low voice. He might have had a gun, probably did, but I didn't see the weapon. All I knew was that when he grabbed her arm, he was taking my mother away from me. And I knew in my heart that I couldn't let her go. If I did, I was afraid I'd never see her again. I jumped into the car with her and held on to her with all my strength."

"You were a gutsy kid."

"Not at all. I was scared out of my head. I heard the men talking in Spanish, trying to figure out how to get rid of me and I yelled at them that I wouldn't leave my mother. They ended up with both of us. Two for the price of one."

"Where did they take you?"

"I curled up on my mom's lap. We put on blindfolds. She pretended it was a game but I knew better. We drove for a long time. When we got out, we were in a fabulous house—a palace, really. They took us up a marble staircase to the third floor. The doors were locked, but we had plenty of space with a bedroom, a sitting room and a bathroom."

"And then?"

"Nothing," she said. "We stayed there for a week. We were well fed and mostly left alone. Then they put on the blindfolds and took us home."

Troy reminded himself that she was telling this story from the perspective of a seven-year-old. Her mother had been there to protect and reassure her child, and he suspected that Olivia's mom had gone through hell during that week. "Tell me about a typical day when you were being held captive."

"I don't think I can remember much detail, but I'll give it a try. First, we'd get up and do some exercises, touching our toes and reaching for the sky. And then, we'd wash up. I had to help my mom because she had a bruise. On her cheek. A huge, dark bruise. Oh, my God."

"What's wrong?"

"I had completely forgotten about the bruise. It was terrible. How could I forget?"

Memory was a funny thing. She hadn't wanted to think of the abduction as a trauma, and she'd suppressed negative thoughts. "How did she get the bruise?"

"Late at night, one of the men came into our room," she said. "He was loud and angry and he smelled bad. His face was red like a devil. And he slapped Mom so hard that she fell on the tile floor."

She inhaled a sharp gasp before continuing. "I

ran to the man. I kicked and I hit and I shoved. I did everything I could to keep him from hurting my mom. And he went away. Mom held me, told me she wasn't really hurt, and we had to be quiet."

His heart ached for the brave little girl who had tried to take care of her mother. "I'm sorry you had to go through that."

"Mom told me to run and hide in the bathroom whenever anybody came into the room, and that's what I did. I stood on the other side of the door and listened really hard. They never hit her again. If they had, I don't know what I would have done." She shook her head. "After a week, we went home."

"Were you ever given an explanation? Did your parents ever talk to you about what happened?"

"Never. We accepted that a bad thing had happened, and we moved on. Literally, we moved. We went to Washington, D.C., for my parents' next assignment."

Because of the kidnapping, their cover story had been compromised. He knew that the Laughton family never returned to South America. Her father had gone on short assignments in Europe and the Middle East. But it wasn't until both of their children graduated from high school and went to college that Richard and Sharon returned to regular work in foreign embassies.

Troy respected her parents for making the

safety of their children a top priority. It was going to be difficult to tell them that their daughter was almost, once again, the victim of a kidnapping. Still, they needed to know. The intruder at Olivia's cabin had taken a photo of the entire family.

THE LODGE-STYLE hotel where he had reservations was four stories tall, and their suite on the top floor had deluxe amenities. After the bellman left her suitcase and his duffel, Troy inspected their space with an eye to security, prowling through the spacious sitting room with its cream-colored leather furniture, the bedroom, bathroom and the tiled area with the hot tub. He positioned a chair in front of the door so anybody breaking in would make a lot of noise, then he stepped onto the balcony that looked toward the moonlit slope. In a few months, the groomed mountainside would be filled with skiers and snowboarders.

Olivia stepped outside and stood beside him at the metal railing. "Are we safe?"

"A determined kidnapper could climb from one balcony to another and get up here. But I think we're okay." He lifted his face to the cool night breeze. "Nice place."

"Very nice."

"When I'm deployed, the conditions are usually awful. I like to treat myself to good hotels."

"With room service," she reminded him.

"Hungry?"

"You can order for me, as long as it's fish, rice, a veggie and maybe a little something sweet."

"A healthy meal for mom and baby." He looked down at her bulging midsection, glad that she was taking good care of their unborn son. "Before you get comfortable, you should call your parents."

"I don't know what to say to them."

She strolled inside, gingerly lowered herself onto the leather sofa and stretched her legs out. Her feet were already bare. She must have kicked off her sneakers as soon as she'd entered the room. In her purple scrubs, her shape reminded him of a ripe eggplant—a comparison he knew he shouldn't mention. They were just beginning to connect, and he didn't want to do anything that would jeopardize his chance to get close to her.

There was one thing all women loved. "Foot rub?" he asked.

"Yes, please."

He sat on the sofa and lifted her feet onto his lap. Her toes were a little puffy. When he took her heel in his hand and gently kneaded her instep, she responded by wriggling herself into a comfy position against the sofa pillows and closing her eyes. Her fingers laced on top of her belly.

As he stroked and rubbed, he studied her face. Seldom had he had the chance to observe her at rest. She was lovely. Though she had dark circles below her eyes, her lightly tanned complexion was flawless—not exactly glowing, but close. Tendrils of blond hair curled alongside her high cheekbones.

"That feels so good." Her lips parted as she made a low, sensual hum. "I *don't* want you to stop, but I *do* want you to call room service."

"You have a call of your own to make," he reminded her.

"Mom and Dad." She sighed. "My father is going to love you. The way you poked around the suite when we came in was exactly what he would do."

Checking the security was a natural instinct for anyone in the intelligence community. "Your dad and I have a few things in common."

"More than a few," she said. "You're a lot like him."

"I doubt that." Troy had seen photos and had read dossiers on the career of Richard Laughton. He was the kind of spy who looked good in a tux and worked in a high-class political arena. "From what I can tell, your father is slick and sophisticated. That's not me."

"And what's your style?"

"Down and dirty," he said.

"But you're both spies. I know that military intelligence is different from the CIA, but you're still gathering information. You're still tracking down the bad guys." As he continued to rub her feet, she kept humming. "What are you working on right now?"

He was making a transition in his work, preparing for the next phase of his career. "Let's just say that it involves a terrorist cell."

"In the United States?"

"That's right."

She wiggled her toes. "Unfortunately, I have to use the bathroom. Can we do more foot rubbing later?"

"As much as you want."

She pulled her feet away from him, sat upright on the sofa and confronted him directly. "I knew from the first time we met you that you were involved in dangerous work."

"Like any soldier," he said with a shrug.

"Like my father."

He met her gaze. Though she was obviously tired, her blue eyes glowed with an inner strength that reminded him of the seven-year-old girl who had fought to protect her mother. Her childhood trauma formed a basis of fear for the adult woman. "You blamed your father when you and your mom were kidnapped."

"It wasn't his fault," she said, quickly defending him.

If she was thinking rationally, she had to know that her father hadn't done anything that he thought would bring danger to his family. After the incident in South America, he'd gone to great lengths to protect them, bringing his wife and daughters to Washington, D.C., to live. Those were the facts.

But reality was always colored by emotion. He imagined that when Olivia thought of kidnapping, she remembered the feelings she'd had as a little girl. At some level, she would hold her father responsible.

"I promise you," he said, "that my work will never endanger you or our child."

She jabbed her forefinger at the center of his chest. "Don't make promises you can't keep."

Her sudden hostility ticked him off. He hadn't yet told her about the changes that were coming up in his career, and he couldn't expect her to know what he was giving up. Nevertheless, she ought to know him well enough to understand that he was, above all, responsible. "What are you getting at?"

"Has it occurred to you that the intruders at my cabin might not be enemies of my parents? They might be someone connected to your terrorist cell."

Somewhere in the back of his mind, he had acknowledged and dismissed that possibility. "They wouldn't know about you. You're not my wife."

"Over the past couple of months, you've sent

me a lot of baby presents, emails and flowers. It wouldn't take a genius to figure out our relationship."

She was right. The attempted kidnapping could be because of his work. It might be his fault that she was in danger.

Chapter Four

After he'd ordered room service and Olivia had retreated to the bedroom to contact her parents, Troy used his secure cell phone to place a call to Gunnery Sergeant Blaine Nelson, who had recently taken Troy's place as the leader for their seven-man special ops team.

Nelson answered his phone with a yawn. It was two hours later at Camp Lejeune on the North Carolina coast but still too early for Nelson to be asleep. Troy wasted no time with pleasantries. "I have a situation."

"Where the hell are you?"

"Wake up, Gunny. I need intel on the whereabouts of the terrorist cell, and I need it now."

"Yes, sir, Captain Weathers, sir."

Troy couldn't help grinning at the overly formal form of address. "What are you trying to tell me, Nelson?"

"That you're being a pain in the butt, sir."

"Duly noted," Troy said. "Give me an update."

"Nothing's changed since this morning when you left. We can't pinpoint locations, but chatter indicates that they're planning their attack in New York City."

"I want you to trace any possible connection to Colorado. There's been a threat."

"No joke? Fill me in." Nelson was now fully alert. He and Troy had worked together for eight years. They were more than associates, more than friends. They were as close as brothers. "What's the nature of this threat?"

"Somebody's after Olivia," he said. "She's had the feeling that she's being watched. About an hour ago, an intruder broke into her cabin. It could be a kidnap attempt."

"Do you think the guys we've been tracking are behind it?"

"I don't know."

Their code name for this terrorist group was Hatari, the Swahili word for *danger,* and they were based in Rwanda. Troy and his team had been responsible for capturing two of their leaders while they were investigating a totally unrelated issue in Africa. If the cell in the U.S. planned to grab Olivia, it could be meant as payback for Troy.

"You said they were tailing her," Nelson said thoughtfully. "That doesn't sound like Hatari."

Troy agreed. The M.O. for these terrorists was

anything but subtle. In their home country, they were responsible for wiping out villages, poisoning wells, burning fields and decimating entire families. They went in with guns blazing, operating under the premise that more firepower was better. If they wanted to threaten him using Olivia, they would have killed her.

But Colorado wasn't their homeland. And the U.S. cell of Hatari was operating under a different set of priorities. They had hooked up with a man whose alias was Kruger—the name he'd used when he'd disappeared off the radar twenty-two years ago. Kruger was under such deep cover that he was nearly transparent. Though he'd lived in the United States, his current identity was unknown. He had no fingerprints on file. There were no existing photographs of him.

"Kruger could be running the show," Troy said. "He might be inclined to pull a kidnapping and use Olivia to force my hand."

"Wish we knew more about him. He's a ghost, an old-school kind of spook."

Similar to Olivia's dad and mom. "I've got to go. Look into the Colorado angle and keep me posted."

"Yes, sir." Nelson yawned again.

"Missing your beauty sleep? It's a little early for you to be hitting the sheets."

"It would be...if I was sleeping alone."

Troy grinned. "Carry on, Gunny."

When Olivia made the call to her parents, it might be smart for him to talk to them, as well. Kruger was something of a legend in CIA circles, and her mom and dad had been part of that inner circle for years. They might have useful advice.

He crossed the sitting room and tapped on the closed bedroom door. "Is it okay for me to come in?"

"Sure thing."

He pushed open the door and stopped dead in his tracks. She'd changed from her hospital scrubs to a long, cream-colored, cotton nightgown with lace and satin ribbons around a neckline that was low enough to showcase her full breasts. The light fabric draped gently over her rounded body. Her golden hair cascaded around her shoulders. She looked like a goddess.

"I thought I'd get changed," she said, "before I made the phone call."

Struck dumb by the abundance of her beauty, he could only stare and nod. This was his woman. She was carrying his child.

She frowned. "What's wrong?"

"Not a thing." He swallowed hard. "You're stunning."

"No need to worry," she joked. "I promise not to knock you over with my giant belly."

"I like the bulge. I like the whole package."

"It's a pretty nightgown. It was a gift from one of my baby showers. I've had four. I guess that's a benefit of being a midwife. Most of the people I know have recently given birth." She swept across the room, majestic as the QEII. At the desk near the window, she picked up her cell phone. "I should probably make this call."

"When you're done, I'd like to speak with your dad."

"Why?"

If circumstances had been different, he would have met her father before he'd asked for her hand in marriage. "The terrorist cell my team is investigating has a CIA crossover. Your dad might have intel I can use."

"Let me get this straight. You want to talk to my dad about spy stuff?"

"He's a source."

"I hadn't planned for you to meet my family." She lowered herself into a padded chair beside the desk. "Certainly not like this."

Though he'd prefer to keep his phone conversation with her father on the level of an intelligence briefing, they couldn't ignore the personal. He and Richard Laughton had more in common than their occupations. "How much have you told them about me?"

Avoiding his gaze, she stared at the phone in

her hand. "They know that you proposed and that I turned you down."

"Did you give them a reason?"

"I tried." She shook her head. "I told them pretty much the same thing I told you. You're a great guy, but we don't have a relationship. And I'm not interested in being married to someone who's always traveling and putting himself in danger on a regular basis."

"What if my career was different?"

She shot him a questioning glance. "Different in what way?"

"What if I wasn't in the field?"

"But you love your work." She rose to her feet and stalked toward him. "Please don't tell me that you've resigned from special ops."

He gave her a weak grin. "Surprise."

"No way. I won't let you quit doing something you love because of me and the baby. That's the worst way to start a relationship. You'd blame me for ruining your life."

He hadn't been expecting her to turn handsprings, but he didn't think she'd be outright hostile. Damn it, this was his decision. His life. "You know, Olivia, not everything is about you."

A knock at the front door to their suite interrupted any further explanation. A voice called out, "Room service."

Before he left the bedroom, Troy drew his gun.

"I'll deal with this. You stay here and make your phone call."

He went to the door and cautiously eased it open. The same bellman who'd carried their suitcases to the suite stood outside with a cart. While Troy watched and kept his weapon hidden behind his back, the young man wheeled into the room and unloaded the plates onto a round table.

Hoping to pick up information, Troy commented, "This must be off-season for the lodge. Are many people staying here?"

"There's a lot more when the ski slopes are open, but you'd be surprised. We get golfers, hikers, mountain bike riders and people who are up here for river rafting."

There wasn't a clever way to ask if the bellman had seen possible Hatari terrorists or a spy named Kruger from the last century. "Mostly families?"

"That's right. And we've got a wedding party coming in tomorrow for the weekend."

Troy gave him a generous tip before he locked the door and shoved a chair in front of it. If he'd been in the field, he never would have tasted food that hadn't been prepared in his sight, but he had no reason to believe Olivia's intruders had followed them to the hotel. He would have noticed a tail.

She emerged from the bedroom. "I talked to my sister and warned her about a possible threat.

After she told me I was nuts, she reminded me that her house has an excellent alarm system. They'll be safe."

He held out his hand for the phone. "Can I talk to your father?"

"Mom and Dad are asleep. They were exhausted after the flight from Cairo, and my sister didn't want to wake them."

"I guess I'll have to wait." He was a patient man, almost to a fault. Patience and persistence were useful traits in his business, but Olivia was straining his reserves. She had a real talent for driving him to the edge and making him want to jump.

He went to the table and lifted the lids off their separate dinners. Pan-fried trout for her. A T-bone steak for him.

As she took her place, she gazed across the table with a guarded expression. "You said the decision to change your career wasn't about me."

"Correct." He sliced into his steak, cut off a chunk and stuffed it into his mouth so he wouldn't have to talk. The consequences of his decision were still painful, and he knew better than to look toward her for understanding.

"I'm listening," she said.

He shrugged. "It's time for a change."

"Is this a military thing? Some kind of requirement?"

"The T-bone's great. How's the fish?"

"Delicious." She poured water from a carafe into her glass and took a sip. "I didn't realize how hungry I was."

"I thought pregnant women were always eating for two."

"Oh, I've done plenty of that. I've packed on thirty-three pounds, probably more than that. I quit weighing myself two days ago." She picked up her fork. "And you're changing the subject. I want to know about your career."

Telling her about the career change was one of the reasons he'd come to Colorado. He was looking at a change in his life that might affect the way she felt about him. From the first time he'd proposed, she had made it crystal clear that she didn't want to be married to a man whose occupation was full of danger and uncertainty. Now that he knew more about her family history, he had a greater understanding of that fear. But he still wouldn't have quit if he hadn't been ready to make the change. As it turned out, the timing was right for him to settle into a different phase of life.

He wanted a home.

He wanted to be a father—a real father, not a part-time visitor.

All he had to do was convince Olivia. It was a risky proposition. If he told her and she still rejected him, he'd know that her reason for avoiding a relationship with him wasn't just his job. She'd be saying no because she didn't like him.

"I'm thirty-six years old," he said. "For somebody who does my kind of work, that's over-the-hill. My reflexes aren't as fast. My aim isn't as sharp as it used to be."

"It sounds like you're being too hard on yourself."

Since he was coming clean, he might as well let her know everything. He left the table and went to his duffel. From a front pocket, he removed a case, took out a pair of silver-rimmed eyeglasses and stuck them on his nose. Wearing them was an admission of declining vision, but it was nice to be able to see the food on the plate. "Right now, I just need them for up close. My long-range vision is okay."

"I like the glasses," she said. "They make you look smart."

He winced. "And it's well-known that a high IQ strikes terror in the hearts of bad guys."

"Is that what you want? To strike terror?"

He shook his head. "I'm still in better shape than ninety percent of the guys out there. That's not my point. I need to be the best, the fastest, the sharpest. Otherwise, I could be putting my men in danger."

"This must be hard for you," she said. "Will you miss the action?"

He thought for a moment before responding. "In spite of what you might think, I'm not an adrenaline junkie. I don't get a thrill from putting my life on the line. My proudest accomplishment as a leader is that I've never lost a man, not a single one in fourteen years. I'm happy to quit while I'm still ahead."

When he looked across the table and met her gaze, he noticed a glow that he'd never seen before. Approval? She smiled gently. "What will you do now?"

"I could continue to go along with my men in a supervisory position, staying behind the lines and giving orders. Or I could opt for a training position at Camp Lejeune. I'd rather be a trainer."

"A desk job?"

"Hell, no. I couldn't handle that. I'll have some time on the training courses and some in the classroom."

As her smile grew brighter, her blue eyes glimmered. Definite approval. He felt like he'd won the lottery. Her voice was warm. "You'll be a good teacher."

"Why do you think so? Is it the glasses?"

"You've got the patience for it." She lifted a forkful of green veggies to her mouth. "You've been able to put up with me for all these months. And I can be pretty stubborn."

"Like a mule."

"But you never gave up," she said. "Even though I said no, you asked again and again and again and—"

"You liked it," he interrupted. "On some level, you liked that I sent flowers for your birthday. You always thanked me."

"Just being polite."

He knew it was more than that, but he didn't push. This dinner was going well. The food was good, and conversation was beginning to come more easily. She talked about what she wanted to do after the baby was born, and they discovered a common interest in rock climbing. He mentioned his interest in historical books and biographies, especially those of presidents and statesmen.

"Do you like politics?" she asked.

"It's not the politics," he said. "It's the strategy that goes into decision making. What do you read?"

"Fiction, all kinds except espionage for obvious reasons. I've been into vampires for a while, but that's not the best kind of book to be reading while I'm sitting with a mom in labor. It's a little too gory." She leaned back in her chair, rested her hands on her bulge and grinned. "This is nice."

"We haven't spent a lot of time like this…just talking."

"Well, we only had two quickie dates before I showed up on your doorstep and pounced."

Things would have been different if they'd gone through a regular courtship. He doubted the outcome would have been the same. From the first time they'd met, there had been physical chemistry, but there had also been logistical obstacles with his international assignments and her mountain lifestyle. There might have been a couple more dates, but they didn't really have a lot in common—not until she'd pounced.

Her cell phone rang, and she picked it up. A frown pulled at the corners of her mouth. "My sister."

"Answer it."

She talked for half a minute. Her frown deepened.

Thrusting the phone toward him, she said, "It's my dad."

Reluctantly, Troy took the call. His relationship with Olivia had progressed more in the past forty-five minutes than it had in eight months. They were enjoying each other's company, growing accustomed to each other.

He was pretty sure that talking to Richard Laughton would change the situation.

Chapter Five

Olivia glared at the closed bedroom door where Troy had retreated for his conversation with her father. Apparently, he needed privacy to discuss how the two of them would handle the potential threat to her life. Heaven forbid that she be consulted.

For most of her life, she'd been proving to her parents that she was an independent woman who was fully capable of managing her own life. Sometimes, Mom got it. But Dad? No way. He still tried to hold her hand when they crossed the street. No doubt, he and Troy would come up with a plan to swaddle her in bubble wrap and lock her away in a fortress until the bad guys were gone.

Not that she blamed them for being protective. She would, of course, do anything necessary to keep herself and the baby safe. But she couldn't let her dad and Troy take over her life, especially not when it came to how she would deliver this baby. This was her area of expertise, and she'd spent a significant chunk of time imagining what it would be like when she was in labor. Her hope was to bring this child into the world in the most natural way possible. The atmosphere would be serene, filled with light and love.

From behind the bedroom door, she heard Troy laughing. The sound grated on her ears. Were they swapping spy stories? Telling secret agent jokes? Exchanging passwords? Though she told herself that it was a good thing for them to get along with each other, she had serious misgivings. If they partnered up, these two could get into all kinds of trouble.

As she cleared the dinner plates off the table onto the room service cart, she thought about Troy's announcement that he was becoming a trainer at Camp Lejeune. His rationale for leaving the front lines of action made sense. It was a life change—*his* life. But what did it mean? What were the further implications? He hadn't actually said that he was going to buy a house near Camp Lejeune and settle down with her and the baby.

In fact, he hadn't proposed since she'd seen him. She didn't think he'd changed his mind about getting married. After all, one of his phone messages said, "Marry me." But he hadn't pushed. Was it possible that he'd finally taken the hint? And why did that make her feel somewhat bereft?

With their room service dinner cleaned up, she

eyeballed the sofa and the huge television screen. If she sat, she might not get up again; maneuvering her weight had become something of an issue. Probably she should skip the sit-down and just crawl into bed. After her long, exhausting day with the triplets, she ought to sleep as soundly as a hibernating grizzly. But she didn't feel tired.

She rested her hands on her belly and felt the baby move. Looking down at the bulge, she asked, "Should I go to bed?"

The kicks were an indecipherable Morse code that she interpreted to mean that the baby wanted her to stay awake for a while. She needed to think about how much danger she was in and about seeing her parents tomorrow and about Troy.

Their dinner conversation had been strangely stimulating. Even with the wire-rimmed glasses, he looked like a man of action—tall and strong with a square, masculine jaw and deep-set, dark eyes that were constantly alert. As they'd talked, he'd allowed her a glimpse of another side to his personality. He'd been a history major in college. He read scholarly books. He was smart and sexy. Who knew?

She went through the door into the corner room with the hot tub. Two of the walls were paneled, and the other two were floor-to-ceiling windows with a sliding glass door. Should she indulge in a soak? Well, why not? Troy was enjoying himself with a spy chat; she might as well do something for herself. She turned on the hot water and went to the bathroom to gather more towels and a white terry cloth robe.

By the time she returned, the tub was half-full. She tested the water. Perfect! She turned off the overhead light, allowing the soft glow of starlight to filter into the room. In the semidark, she could see the outline of pine trees outside the windows. With her long hair twisted into a knot on top of her head, she slipped out of her nightgown and lowered herself into the warm, soothing liquid.

The tub was large enough for her to stretch out prone with her head at one end and her feet at the other. Her belly and breasts bobbed on the surface of the water like round, white islands. As soon as the water was high enough, she activated the jets and positioned her back against the massaging gush of water. Pure relaxation spread through her.

The door behind her opened, and Troy asked, "May I come in?"

"As long as you don't turn on the lights."

Moving closer, he leaned his elbows on the edge of the hot tub. Moonlight fell across his wide shoulders and glistened in his dark hair. Since she could see him clearly, she knew he could see her, too. Even with the swirling water, he'd be able to make out her naked outline below the water. A little embarrassing but not enough that she was going to worry about it.

"What did you and my dad talk about?"

"How much do you want to know?"

"Everything," she said firmly. Her parents had never told her and her sister about their work, probably because it was top secret and they were just kids. But this situation was different. She was a grown woman with her own unborn child to protect. "The more I know, the better I'll feel."

"It's a long story. Mind if I join you?"

Sharing a bath might lead to physical intimacy, which was something she'd avoided since the night she got pregnant. Other women had told her how they were sexually supercharged during pregnancy, but that hadn't been her experience. Not yet, anyway.

She shrugged. "Suit yourself."

When he peeled off his T-shirt, her pulse rate bumped into high gear. The starlight through the window shone on the sharp ridges of his muscular arms and shoulders. Dark hair sprinkled across his chest and narrowed down the center of his body, pointing toward his belt buckle. He unfastened the belt and shucked off his jeans.

"I'm going to open the sliding glass door," he said. "I like the feeling of cool air and hot water."

"Sure."

Without a hint of modesty, he walked around

the tub to the windows. Naked, completely naked, he was spectacular. She couldn't help staring at him. When he pushed the door open, a breeze wafted inside and cooled her cheeks, which was a very good thing because she was on fire.

Troy slipped into the hot tub. On the opposite side, he was far enough away that they weren't touching, but if she stretched out her legs, her feet would bump into his knees.

He ducked under the water and bobbed to the surface again, shaking his head and grinning. "Feels good."

"Uh-huh." She tried to look away but couldn't.

"Our bad guy's name is Kruger," he said. "That's his alias, anyway."

She clenched her hands into fists, fighting to control the passionate urges that coursed through her. She needed to concentrate; his information was important. "You referred to our bad guy. Yours and my dad's? Are you both looking for the same person?"

"Not exactly. Your dad, like everybody else in the CIA, is after Kruger. He's a legendary deep-cover agent—a sleeper. For nearly twenty-two years, he's lived in the United States and hidden behind an undercover identity. It's likely that he's in a position of power. Your dad is aware of him but hasn't been directly involved."

"And how do you know Kruger?"

"My team discovered evidence of a terrorist cell from Rwanda that's operating in the U.S., probably near New York. The group calls itself Hatari, and it's being financed by Kruger."

Espionage wasn't her thing. Cells and sleepers and terrorist plots were beyond her sphere of influence. "How does this affect me?"

"We don't know." He swept his arm across the surface of the water, sending a shimmering ripple toward her. "At this point, all we can do is conjecture. Since I'm the leader of the group that found out about the Hatari plot, they might think they can influence me by kidnapping you. Or Kruger might want to get the attention of the CIA through your father."

"Convoluted."

"Very," he agreed. "I picked up one potentially useful fact from your dad. According to the CIA, Kruger is involved with the oil business."

"And why is that useful?"

"It gives a possible focus for our target. If the Hatari plot is to blow up a building, Kruger might direct them toward the offices of one of his business rivals."

"In New York?"

"As far as we know." He eased through the water, moving closer to her. "And there are a lot of oil companies who have offices in Colorado. Kruger might be closer than we think."

"What should we do?"

"I'm not taking any chances." He was beside her with his hand resting on her shoulder. "Until this is over, I'm not letting you out of my sight."

His neatly trimmed hair was slick and wet like a seal. She reached up to stroke his temple. If she wanted to avoid getting close to him, she should climb out of the tub right now. Instead, her hand slid down to his nape, and she gazed into the depths of his dark eyes. "You haven't asked me to marry you since we've been together."

"Your dad gave me his blessing."

"Oh, no, you didn't." Annoyed, she dropped her hand and pushed away from him.

"Actually, I—"

"I can't believe you asked him." Her irritation mounted. "And he gave you permission. What is this? The Middle Ages?"

"I didn't mention marriage." He pursued her through the water. "He said that you told him I proposed, and he thought it was a good idea for us to be married."

"Of course he did." She splashed him. "My father doesn't think a woman can be complete without a man."

He splashed her back. "Not just any man. Richard approves of me. He researched my background."

"Just like you did with him."

"Guilty," he said.

"Well, I hope you two spies live happily ever after." She groped at the side of the hot tub, trying to lay hands on her towel. "I'm out of here."

"Wait." He caught hold of her arm. "I've got a different kind of proposal. It's not about getting married."

She bobbed away from him, keeping her distance. "What is it?"

"We've never really gotten to know each other. When we talked over dinner, I think that was the longest sustained conversation we've ever had."

"So?"

"While I'm acting as your bodyguard, we have to stay together. Let's use this time. It'll be a courtship."

"A courtship?" She couldn't help smiling when he used that old-fashioned word. A professor or a nerd might refer to dating as courtship, but Troy was a studly marine intelligence guy whose muscles had muscles. "Do you intend to woo me?"

"I could woo."

"And why does that sound dirty?"

"I want to spend time with you, and I promise not to bring up the topic of marriage. No stress. No pressure."

She didn't make the mistake of thinking that this proposal came without a concession on her part. "And what do you want from me?"

"I want to be with you when you give birth. I want to see my son being born."

His request touched her. A lot of men went running when they thought of a woman in labor. The mere fact that he wanted to participate said good things about his character. Still, she clung to her suspicions. "This had better not be some kind of ploy to get me into a hospital. I have a very clear idea of how I want this baby to be born."

He nodded. "You're the boss."

"Well, I can't say no. It feels right to have both parents at the birth. We have a deal."

"And now we seal it with a kiss."

He dragged her through the water into an embrace. Their wet bodies slid against each other until he found a position that worked. He held her sideways against his chest. As they kissed, her resistance washed away. Her tongue probed against the firm line of his mouth, and he opened his lips. His tongue engaged with hers.

She floated against him with the swirling water caressing her skin. The cool breeze through the open door prickled the hairs on her arms. She couldn't believe how ultrasensitive her body felt. When he touched her swollen breast, it was almost painful but also felt so good.

His lips nuzzled her ear. "You're beautiful."

"I'm huge."

"Ripe," he said.

He pushed her through the water until her back was pressed against one of the jets. The gushing water massaged the region of her lumbar vertebrae, easing the stiffness that came from standing all day. While her muscles released the tension of being overtired, a whole catalog of other sensations came to life. Troy knew exactly where to kiss for the greatest response. His caresses were gentle, but he was clearly in control as he shifted his touch from her breast to the inside of her thigh. If this was his idea of courtship, she was ready for more woo-woo-woo.

Without warning, he cinched his hands under her arms and lifted her. He stood in the hot tub, holding her aloft. Her belly was completely out of the water.

"What are you doing?" She smacked him on top of his head. "Put me down."

"Right here." He sat her on the edge of the tub. "I want to see you."

The breeze through the window raised goose bumps on her skin as he moved in close for another kiss. She wrapped her arms around him. The feel of his sleek, wet, muscular backside aroused her even more.

As he glided her back into the warm water, he parted her legs. Gently, he stroked her, and she felt herself coming undone. She hadn't expected this to happen, hadn't thought she'd see fireworks behind her closed eyelids, hadn't dreamed of this passionate release that sent shock waves through her entire body.

He gathered her into his arms, and she rested her head on his shoulder. Making love had never been this amazing.

They floated for a moment before he helped her out of the tub and toweled her dry. When she reached for her nightgown, he took it away from her. "You don't need that. I'll keep you warm tonight."

"My hair." She reached up to touch the damp tendrils that had fallen from the ponytail.

"It'll dry."

In the bedroom, he pulled back the linens on the king-size bed. When they'd first entered the suite, she'd intended to discuss the sleeping arrangements with him and to request that he sleep on the sofa's fold-out bed, but that seemed ridiculous now. She slipped between the sheets, and he joined her, nestling against her backside with his hand resting possessively on her belly.

It occurred to her that their passion had been one-sided. She'd gotten all the pleasure and really ought to reciprocate. Before she could make a move, a sweet lethargy overcame her and she slept.

Chapter Six

In the morning, Troy was awakened by a kiss and a not-so-subtle caress. Without opening his eyes, he responded, sliding his hand over the lush contour of her belly. Her skin was smooth and slightly moist, reminding him of the hot tub.

"Don't make a move," she whispered. "I want to give you a very special start to the day."

"But I like to move."

"And how do you like this?" She raked her fingernails down his chest to his belly button and lower.

"Keep going," he growled.

This was, without doubt, the number one best wake-up call he'd ever had in his life. *Give the lady a trumpet and let her play reveille.* He kept his eyes closed, using his sensory memory to record every kiss, every caress and every stroke. He memorized her scent and the taste of her sweet lips. When she'd driven him nearly crazy, he returned the favor.

Afterward, they lay side by side on the king-size bed, breathing hard and very happy. When it came to sexual compatibility, they were a good couple. No, make that a great couple. They had chemistry out the wazoo. Not a bad foundation for a relationship.

He turned his head and opened his eyes to study her profile. Her nose, though small, was well-defined. The corners of her mouth naturally turned up, and when she smiled, her eyes crinkled. He didn't know her expressions well. Watching her was still a revelation to him.

"It's after eight o'clock," she said. "I told my sister that we'd be in Denver for lunch."

The drive from Keystone was a couple of hours, but he was in no hurry to get moving. Swimming through the undercurrent of tension between Olivia and her parents wasn't going to be fun. Plus, Troy was uncomfortable about being the guy who was responsible for getting Olivia pregnant before they'd even had a real date.

Hoping he might find an ally in her family, he asked, "What's your sister like?"

"Bianca is the favorite daughter who does everything right. She graduated from Yale Law at the top of her class, and she's a third-year associate at one of the most prestigious firms in Denver. Last year, she bought a terrific house with some help on the down payment from my parents."

"You mentioned her boyfriend."

"He's out of the picture." She shrugged her shoulders. "Us Laughton girls don't seem to do well with long-term, committed relationships."

Lying on his side, he propped his head on his fist, enjoying the rolling view of her belly and breasts under the sheets. "How come?"

"Bianca would say my problem is being a hermit who hides in her mountain lair every time she sees a man coming. And I'd say she's a lawyer, trained to pick everything apart."

He didn't think of Olivia as a hermit. She'd come to him on the night they'd made a baby. Since then, she'd avoided him, rejected his proposals and made it clear that she was a totally independent woman.

Though he didn't understand, he wasn't ready to go that deep this morning. Things between them were going well, and he wanted to keep it that way. "Why do you think your sister is the favorite?"

"Our parents had high expectations. They truly believe that their girls are destined for greatness. When I showed an interest in medicine, they assumed I'd become a doctor. They don't understand why I chose to be a midwife." She turned her head to look at him. Her blue eyes held a challenge. "Do you?"

"Do I what?" He had the sense that he was walking into a minefield.

"Do you understand why I'd want to be a midwife?"

He considered for a moment. If he answered wrong, she'd lump him into the category of insensitive jerks. "I know you like helping people. That's why you volunteer with my brother at the clinic. I think, for you, being a midwife is a calling."

She nodded. "What else?"

"Delivering babies usually has a positive outcome. I get that part, for sure. At the end of labor, you get to be with a happy mother and a brand-new infant. That sounds like a great job to me."

She rewarded him with a smile. "You're smarter than you look."

"What's that supposed to mean?"

"A guy who's as pretty as you shouldn't—"

He gave a snort. "Don't call me pretty."

"Let's just say that you don't look like a nerd." She leaned toward him and kissed his forehead. "Can we call room service? I'm starved."

They took their time getting ready, lingering over the menu and talking and eating. Though they seemed to be settling into a comfortable pattern, she started getting twitchy and tense when it came time to get dressed. Finding the right outfit to meet her parents seemed to be a real big deal, and she changed clothes a half dozen times.

It was after ten when they checked out. Outside, he crossed the small parking area at the front of the resort and unlocked the back of a new rental SUV for the bellman. While their suitcases were being stowed in the back, Troy went around to the passenger side to open the door for her.

"What are you doing?" Her gaze was puzzled. "This isn't our car."

"It is now. Range Rover SUV. It's a decent ride."

After he got behind the wheel and drove toward the exit from the lot, he felt her staring at him, staring hard. When she spoke, her tone was cold. "Aren't you going to tell me why we changed cars?"

"A precaution," he said. "I didn't notice anybody following us last night, but that doesn't mean there's no more threat. The intruders might have spotted our vehicle. Last night, while our rental SUV was parked, they could have planted a bug or a tracking device. So I contacted the rental place and got a replacement. This Range Rover is clean."

"Seems paranoid," she muttered.

"It's called strategy. Being one step ahead of your opponent."

He loved strategy. After he retired, he'd probably turn into a Civil War reenactor or one of those guys who built miniature models of Napoleon's defeat at Waterloo. Unfortunately, in the current situation, he didn't have a whole lot of options when it came to planning strategic maneuvers.

Troy usually worked with trained troops. Protecting a pregnant woman was a whole different story. He couldn't take risks to draw the bad guys into the open; his focus was to avoid potential danger.

"From now on," she said, "I want to be in the loop. I want to know your plans before you make a decision."

"I'll keep you informed, but these decisions aren't up for discussion."

"Why not?" Her voice took on an edge of irritation. "Don't I get to have a say?"

"Chain of command doesn't work that way." As soon as the words left his mouth, he knew he'd made a mistake.

"Command?" Her jaw tensed. "Who do you think you are? The master and commander?"

"I'm trying to protect you."

"Just like my dad. Trying to run my life and pretending it's for my own good."

There was no point in arguing with this stubborn woman. He shifted the subject. "Which route should we take to Denver?"

"The Eisenhower Tunnel is faster," she said

tersely. "We'd have to drive back to Dillon to get on the interstate."

Returning to Dillon was counterintuitive. Even if they'd managed to lose the intruders who broke into her cabin, the bad guys could still be hanging around and watching the roads. "We're closer to Loveland Pass."

"And it's a prettier drive."

The old road that climbed over the Continental Divide was a more likely place for an ambush—a less-traveled route with a lot of twists and hairpin turns. He sat at the stop sign. Left or right? Dillon or the pass? Brilliant summer sunshine lit up the forests and glinted against windshields of other vehicles. On a day like this, it was hard to believe that someone might be following them.

"If you're worried about driving the mountain roads," she said with phony sweetness, "I'd be delighted to take over the wheel."

He could have told her about his extensive training in defensive driving techniques or his escape in a Hummer across the rugged terrain in Afghanistan or the time he went over a hundred and twenty miles per hour in a Ferrari on the German autobahn. But there was no need to brag. "I can handle Loveland Pass."

Taking the high road turned out to be a good plan. The panoramic mountain views seemed to calm her nerves. After they crested the summit, he tried to ease himself back into her good graces. "I like the outfit you're wearing."

"It's too plain."

He heard a grinding note of hostility and proceeded with caution. "You made a good choice. It'll be hot in Denver. You're practical to wear shorts."

"Here's a hint, Troy. Telling a woman that her clothes are practical isn't a compliment."

"The colors are nice and bright," he said. "I like the black-and-yellow striped top. You remind me of a bumblebee."

"Again, not a compliment."

He tried again. "The way the material drapes—"

"Over my giant belly?" She was determined to find fault with anything he said. "My massive, watermelon belly?"

"Damn it, Olivia. What do you want me to say?"

"You don't have to flatter me. I know I'm gross and pregnant. Either tell me the truth or be quiet."

"Here's the truth," he said tersely. "You look sexy as hell. Your bare legs are tan and firm and I want to lick from your toes to your hips. That shirt gives me a peek at your cleavage—your amazing cleavage. And that round, beautiful belly turns me on."

Her lower lip trembled. Three small gasps turned into a sob. "Thank you."

"Are you crying?"

"No."

But she was. Crying. Damn. "All right, I take it all back. I'm sorry."

"Not your fault." She raked her fingers through her long hair and shook her head. "It's the hormones."

His fingers clenched on the steering wheel. The rocky slopes and distant peaks faded into the background as he stared at her. She was the center of his world. "Does this happen often, this crying thing?"

Her hiccupping sob turned into a giggle. Was it possible to be crying and laughing at the same time? She swabbed her cheeks and looked at him. "Yes, I have these unreasonable outbursts. And I can't really tell you if they're going to get better or worse. I've never been eight and a half months pregnant before."

"Is it the stress?" he asked.

"Could be. Seeing my parents is never easy."

"I was talking about the possible kidnapping."

Her lips spread in a grin. "Oh, yeah. That, too."

Her smile worried him. He didn't think she took the potential for danger seriously. Hell, he didn't understand her at all.

ON I-70 APPROACHING Denver, Troy checked his rearview mirror for the third time in as many minutes. Shortly after they'd passed the Evergreen exit, he'd noticed two vehicles staying in close proximity to their Range Rover. One was a black SUV. The other, a sedan with dark tinted windows.

"Something wrong?" Olivia asked.

"It's hard to tell on the highway. I'm going to slow down and see who stays with us."

His foot eased off the accelerator, and their speed dropped to forty-three miles per hour. The SUV passed them on the left, moving too fast for Troy to catch a glimpse of the driver. The sedan hung back on their tail.

Olivia twisted around in the seat to see out the back window. "That car with the tinted windows hasn't speeded up. Do you think he's following us?"

"I had my eye on that car and the SUV that just went by. I might have been wrong about him."

Three miles down the road, he spotted the SUV parked on the shoulder. As they passed, he pulled out to follow them.

"That's the SUV," Olivia said. "You weren't wrong."

The use of two vehicles usually indicated a plan for a pincer-type maneuver. One would move in front of them while the other closed in on their rear. In a synchronized move, both cars would slow, forcing Troy to stop. But a four-lane highway with other traffic wasn't a good place for that move. These two cars could be maintaining contact to keep an eye on them. "This could just be a coincidence. These cars could be headed to Denver like we are."

"Or not," she said.

He needed to find out if this was purposeful surveillance. "I'm getting off at the next exit. We'll see what they do."

Maintaining the legal speed limit, Troy turned the steering wheel, swerved without signaling and drove onto the exit ramp. The sedan trailed behind their Range Rover.

"He's still there," Olivia said.

"Can you see the SUV?"

"Not yet."

The exit dumped them into the outskirts of Denver—a good thing because it meant they weren't in a deserted area. The downside was that the sedan could have a legitimate reason to take this route. At the first intersection, Troy drove into a suburban development with beige two-story houses, nice lawns and skimpy trees.

The sedan stayed with them as Troy made a series of turns and double-backs through the development. At one quiet corner, Olivia warned, "I see the SUV."

His doubts about surveillance disappeared.

These two vehicles were purposely staying close. "Hang on tight."

"What are you going to do?"

"Lose them."

He drove out of the development. With the SUV creeping up on his tail, he punched the gas and took off. On the two-lane road through the foothills, there was just enough traffic to make it difficult for their pursuers. He dodged around a truck and another SUV. The Range Rover was going over sixty as they approached an intersection with a stoplight. It turned amber.

He couldn't race straight through. There were too many other cars waiting for the light to change; they'd be broadsided.

The light was red. He hit the brake, simultaneously cranked the steering wheel and slammed into a right turn, barely avoiding collision.

In the rearview mirror, he saw their pursuers get stuck at the light. This was his chance to put some serious distance between them. The Range Rover flew down the road. This SUV handled nicely for a heavy vehicle on a solid wheelbase. If he could make it to the next turn, they'd be in the clear.

"Olivia, are you okay?"

"Fine." Her voice was a squeak.

"I promise not to do that again."

"Good."

He heard the wail of a police siren. Red-and-blue lights flashed behind the Range Rover. There was no choice but to stop. He pulled onto the shoulder.

"Do we tell the police what's happening?" she asked.

Explaining surveillance and attempted kidnapping would be complicated. Since Troy wasn't officially on a mission, he didn't really have the authority to drive like a maniac. "I'd rather not."

"No problem," she said. "Leave this to me."

When the patrolman appeared at their window, Olivia let out a ferocious scream. "My God," she yelled. "The baby's coming."

Covering his own surprise, Troy looked at the startled cop. "My wife is in labor."

"Now." Olivia flailed. She arched her back and her belly heaved impressively. "It's coming now."

"We're headed to St. Luke's," Troy said.

Olivia grabbed his arm and peered up at the cop. Her face was flushed. Her voice was desperate. "Help me, please."

The cop leaned into the car. "No need to worry, ma'am. I can handle the delivery."

"No," Troy said sharply. "She needs a hospital."

"With all due respect, I have training."

"Triplets!" Olivia shouted. "I'm having three babies."

The cop took an involuntary step back. His jaw dropped. His face went pale. “Three?”

“We need to get to the hospital fast,” Troy said.

“Right,” the cop said. “Follow me.”

Olivia continued her wailing until the police car pulled in front of them. With lights flashing, he led the way into the city, cutting through traffic.

She gave him a grin. “Scared you, didn’t I?”

“What made you think of it?”

“Going into labor?” She patted her bulge. “Let’s just say it’s been on my mind.”

Duh. He should have known.

She continued, “I probably should have run my plan by you. Keeping to the chain of command and all.”

“I think we both know who’s really in charge.”

In his mind, he filled his own name into that blank. He was the boss. He was pretty sure she felt the same way about herself.

Chapter Seven

Olivia felt a twinge of guilt about using her pregnancy to trick a law enforcement officer into escorting them. She didn't like lying, especially not to a nice policeman who had offered to deliver her baby at curbside. Still, the end result was worth a fib. They'd gotten away from the bad guys.

On their escorted ride into town, Troy had called his brother, who worked in the emergency room at St. Luke's when he wasn't at the clinic. Alex had met them at the E.R. with a wheelchair, pretending to be her doctor. After he dismissed the officer and pretended to handle the paperwork, the three of them sneaked out of the hospital. They stood on the sidewalk beside the Range Rover.

Alex grumbled, "Every time you two get together, things get crazy."

"Crazy in a good way," Troy said. "You're happy about your nephew, right?"

"Don't change the subject. Tell me, what the hell is going on?"

It was easy to see that these two men were brothers. They were both tall and lean. Both had brown eyes and black hair. Troy had a darker complexion, and his features were weathered and craggy. Alex wore his hair longer, and his face was thinner. Though she couldn't say why, other than his blue scrubs, she thought Alex looked like a doctor. His expression seemed questioning, sincere and concerned. Troy radiated sheer masculine confidence.

"Long story short," Troy said. "Olivia is in danger, and I'm protecting her."

"From what?"

"Don't know for sure."

Alex scoffed. "That's a cover. It's what you always say."

"How about if I tell you that she might be the target of a Rwandan terrorist cell working for a master spy?"

"Yeah, sure." Alex turned his attention to her. "How are you feeling when you're not faking labor?"

"I'm great, ready to pop. My real labor could be starting any time now. Until then I'd like to stay active. Is it okay for me to stop by the clinic while I'm in town?"

"That's a great idea. Some of the women have

been asking about you." He cocked his head to one side. "And there's somebody I want you to talk to."

"Who's that?"

"Carol Rainer."

Olivia cringed inside. Carol Rainer was a former client, not someone she wanted to see again but someone she couldn't ignore. "How did you run into Carol?"

"She's working at the clinic as a receptionist."

Olivia never would have expected the very wealthy Mrs. Rainer to be involved with the homeless. "How did that happen?"

"Because of you," he said. "You mentioned the clinic, and she stopped by to check us out. At first, she was planning to make a donation and move on, but we were busy that day. She got swept up in the action and decided she liked it."

Of all the people in the world, Carol had the most reason to hate Olivia. They'd been through hell together. "Is she happy?"

"Seems to be."

"And her husband?"

"He's not in the picture anymore." Alex glanced back at his brother. "Are you staying at my house?"

"Probably not. Olivia's parents are in town, and I hope to stay with her sister."

"You should join us for dinner," she said. "I

can't believe I haven't introduced you to Bianca. She's single. A lawyer."

As soon as she spoke, she regretted the invitation. Olivia knew better than to set up her sister on blind dates. Bianca hated being manipulated as much as she did.

"We should go," Troy said.

"Hold on." His brother exhaled a long-suffering sigh. "Call me if you need anything. You're both nuts, but I want you to know that I'm here for you. And for my nephew. I have a feeling that the kid is going to need a sane, stable presence in his life."

Troy grinned. "Every boy needs a stodgy, boring uncle."

"Have you picked out a name?"

The question made her nervous. There were so many decisions she'd been putting off. It had taken her a week to choose the shade of blue she used to paint the nursery, which she was reconsidering even now. Blue for a boy seemed too mundane. "I've been thinking about names. Nothing seems right. I guess I'll know when I see him for the first time."

"Please tell me you're not going to look out a window and name him after the first thing you see. I don't want my nephew to be named Cloudy Sky or Lodgepole Pine."

"I promise," she said.

After hugging Alex, she got into the car and they headed toward her sister's house in south Denver. She had a lot to think about, starting with Carol Rainer, who used to live in a fabulous home in Dillon. Now she was in Denver? Taking care of the homeless? Olivia actually wasn't too surprised that she'd split from her husband who was an aggressive, loud, arrogant businessman. Carol was way too good for him.

It would be painful to see Carol after what had happened eight and a half months ago. Olivia absently stroked her belly. This might not be the best time. Carol had lost her baby.

Olivia realized that neither she nor Troy had spoken for several blocks. She glanced over at him. "You're being awfully quiet."

"Thinking," he said. "I can't help wondering how they located us. We didn't stop for gas, and we weren't followed when we were driving over the pass. They couldn't have planted a tracking device on the Range Rover."

"You said that you noticed them near Evergreen," she said. "They must have been waiting and watching."

"I changed cars. They didn't know what we were driving. Sure, there are traffic cams along the highway, but it's unlikely that they could check out every vehicle."

"Does it matter?"

He stopped at a red light and turned toward her. "They had to be using some kind of GPS tracking device. If it's not on the car, it's with you."

Before they'd left her cabin, he'd gone through her things to make sure the bad guys hadn't planted a bug or a locating device. "You searched my stuff. You even took my cell phone apart to deactivate the GPS."

"I must have missed it."

From his tone, she could tell that he was angry. Not at her but at himself. She tried to reassure him. "It's okay. We'll find it."

"They could be tracking us right now, watching from street corners, following from a few blocks behind."

The hairs on the back of her neck prickled. She didn't like the idea that she was under surveillance. "If that's true, we're leading them straight to my sister's house."

"I'm sure they've already got that location," he said. "They might have stolen a snapshot of your family to see what they look like, but it's no secret that you have a sister in Denver. Finding her address is child's play."

"Will they be watching us at her house?"

"Count on it."

A shudder went through her. She wasn't scared but apprehensive. Like the feeling she had when hiking through a cattle pasture, sooner or later she was going to step into something stinky. But this misstep was far more dangerous than a cow pie.

They continued driving south, passing the gold steeple of the Ritchie Center at the University of Denver. She realized that she'd felt this sort of apprehension before. After she and her mom had been kidnapped, Olivia had been constantly vigilant. Every person she encountered seemed suspicious. She was always waiting for the moment when somebody would step from the shadows and grab her. "I don't like this."

"Me, neither." His jaw tensed. "I'm on my way to meet a legendary spy couple, and the first thing I have to tell them was that I couldn't find a lousy GPS locator."

"What?"

"Your dad can find what I missed. He probably travels with a sweeper to check for bugs and other devices."

"And that's what you're worried about?"

"Well, yeah. I want to make a good first impression."

"As a spy?" Never mind her fear or the danger to her and the baby or the development of their relationship. "You want my father to think you're as good as he is."

"I just don't want him to see me as a total incompetent."

Hot rage flashed through her. She was a furnace, burning with fiery embers. "What about me? And the baby? Don't you care about us?"

"Why are you angry?" He had the audacity to look surprised. "You're my number one concern. You know that."

"Do I?"

"You and our son are the center of my world. It kills me that I screwed up and put you in danger."

"And my father?"

"Nobody else's opinion is as important to me as yours. Understand? Nobody else."

Her anger began to subside. "You better remember that."

He reached over to touch her arm. "Are you okay? Your face is kind of red."

"Hormones," she snapped, even though she knew her anger was more than a hormonal response. She hadn't expected to be taking Troy to meet her parents, hadn't planned on being thrust into danger. "Alex might be right. When we're together, things get crazy."

"In a good way." His smile was gentle and consoling. "Together, we created a miracle."

"Yes, we did." Her hand rested on her belly. She couldn't stay angry at Troy when he said something so right.

HER SISTER ANSWERED before the doorbell finished chiming the opening bars to "Camelot." Olivia had her guard up. She sailed into the entryway with a suitable grand gesture. "Troy, this is Bianca, and this is her starter mansion. Apart from the marble foyer, the Waterford Crystal chandelier and the grand staircase, it's not too flashy. Only four bedrooms plus office but the neighborhood is top-notch."

Bianca shook his hand. "I'm so happy to meet the man who lured my hermit sister out of her cave. Tell me, did you use raw meat or did you just club her over the head and drag her out by her hair?"

Though his posture was military and erect, his grin came easy. "To tell the truth, Olivia was the one who did the clubbing and dragging."

"Never thought my sister had such good taste." She leaned down to talk to Olivia's belly. "And how's my little nephew? I haven't seen you for a month. He's gotten huge."

"And active," she said. "Go ahead. You can touch."

Her sister placed both hands on her bulge. When she felt a kick, she gasped. "Oh, my God, Olivia. We're going to have a baby."

When Bianca threw both arms around her neck and hugged, Olivia felt glad tears welling behind her eyelids. This was the way family was supposed to be—happy and sharing in the joy of a new life. Through the years, she and her sister had their differences, but they were still close.

Before her tears could spill, she saw her parents. Her tall, slim father wore a navy blazer with gold buttons. His white hair was swept back from his high forehead. Her mom was dressed in beige jersey slacks and a matching sleeveless top with a gold belt. They looked like a portrait of royalty from a bygone era, but her mother's face was animated as she rushed to join in the hug.

She whispered, "I've been so worried. Are you all right?"

"I'm fine."

"I can't believe this is happening to you."

"Again," Olivia said.

Her mother pulled away sharply. Her blue eyes—the same azure-blue as both of her daughters—confronted her directly. As a rule, they never discussed her childhood kidnapping. It simply wasn't something they talked about. Olivia couldn't imagine their relationship without the veil of secrecy that had always kept her mom at a distance.

Her mom's mouth fell into a prim smile. "Aren't you going to introduce me to your young man?"

Troy and her dad had already clasped hands and introduced themselves. The two men regarded each other suspiciously, each taking the measure of the other. Olivia had the distinct impression that they were friendly but also adversarial.

"Troy, this is my mom."

"Please call me Sharon," she said as she clasped his hand in both of hers. "Can I offer you coffee? We could all sit down at the table. Lunch is almost ready."

"Pleased to meet you both," Troy said. "Before we do anything else, we need to talk about the attempted abduction. Olivia and I were followed on our way into Denver. We should take protective measures."

"Really?" Bianca's eyes went wide.

"There's a definite threat," Troy said.

Her parents exchanged a glance, clearly uncomfortable with this topic. Olivia couldn't have been more pleased with the way Troy slashed through the aura of civility and got down to business. "Bianca, what kind of security do you have?"

"The best," her sister assured her. "It's a sensor system that alerts us to any disturbance from a broken window to somebody jiggling a doorknob."

"Dead bolt on the door," Troy noted. He looked toward the long windows on either side of the door. "Triple-pane windows?"

"All through the house," Bianca said. "I had them installed for insulation but they're also bulletproof."

"What about the fence?" Troy asked.

"The back fence is wired, but I never use the system. It gets triggered too easily. The alarm goes off if the neighbor's dog pees against it or if the wind blows a tree branch too close."

"Now would be a good time to activate that alarm." Troy looked toward her parents. "I'm guessing that you're armed."

"Yes," her dad said tersely.

Olivia noticed that her mother gave an almost imperceptible nod. "Mom? Are you packing heat?"

"No way," Bianca said.

With her prim smile firmly fixed in place, Sharon Laughton lifted her beige jersey pant leg to show a holster strapped to her slender ankle. "Your father and I need to discuss the situation with Troy. You girls should go into the kitchen and finish the preparations for lunch."

"You can't brush us out of the way," Olivia said. "The intruder at my house took a snapshot of all of us. Whether you like it or not, Bianca and I are both involved."

"My dear," her dad said, "it's not appropriate."

"I insist. I want to hear what's going on."

"Not appropriate," her mother echoed. Though she was still smiling, there was a ring of steel in her voice. "Olivia, I'm sure you understand."

"Not really. This threat could be because of

some sleeper spy you knew back in the day. Bianca and I have a right to know."

"That's not exactly true," Bianca said. "You and I don't have authorization to hear what they're talking about. It's a matter of security clearance."

Olivia would not be brushed aside. "It's a matter of trust. Our family has been threatened. Your grandson."

"I agree." Troy's voice was deep and steady. "In order to protect Olivia, she needs to know what to watch for. I suggest we start with our luggage. I don't have the equipment to check for bugs or GPS location devices."

Richard arched an eyebrow. His eyes were a light blue, almost opaque, and his gaze was intense.

Olivia had no idea how her dad would react. Very few people stood up to him, but Troy's attitude made it clear that he had no intention of backing down. Either these two would be on the same page or they'd be at each other's throats.

"I have the necessary equipment upstairs," Richard said. "Troy and I will go out to the car and check the luggage to make sure we take care of the bugs. Then we'll join you ladies in the dining room for lunch. At that time, we'll discuss our current situation. Is that satisfactory to everyone?"

He was looking directly at her. Olivia gave a nod. "Fine with me."

She watched as the two men ascended the sweeping staircase to the second-floor bedrooms. She was gratified by the way Troy had taken her side. Having him with her changed the family dynamic. She wasn't alone anymore.

Chapter Eight

In the kitchen, Olivia wasn't surprised to see five perfect quiches sitting in a row on the shining black marble surface of a long counter that separated the cooking area from a casual dining area and family room. Quiche was her sister's specialty—one of the few dishes this busy lawyer knew how to cook.

Bianca pivoted and confronted her. "Wow."

"Excuse me?"

"I said wow. Does he have a brother?"

"As a matter of fact, he does."

A smile played on Bianca's lips. She was a few inches shorter than Olivia and slender as a greyhound. Her blond hair was expertly streaked and professionally tousled in a chin-length bob. "Is this brother also tall, dark and handsome?"

"You bet, and he's a doctor."

"Perfect." She looked toward their mom, who had gone straight to the refrigerator and was taking out veggies for a green salad. "What do you think, Mom? Should I meet this handsome doctor?"

"Why ask me? You girls haven't paid the least bit of attention to my advice on boyfriends since you packed away your teddy bears."

"That doesn't mean we don't care about your opinion," Bianca said. "I think Troy is amazing, don't you?"

Holding her breath, Olivia waited for the response. Her mom wasn't the sort of woman who lavished praise on anyone or anything. She could scrutinize a ten-carat diamond and see only the flaw. Cool and reserved, Sharon Laughton arrayed the veggies on the countertop beside the stainless steel sink and took a paring knife from a drawer.

Without turning around, she said, "Troy seems to be a man who knows what he wants."

Olivia stared at the back of her mother's head, trying to discern the underlying meaning in her words. "Could be his Marine Corps training."

"He asked you to marry him, didn't he?"

"Yes."

She sliced open an avocado and removed the pit. "Why did you turn down his proposal?"

"Because I hardly know him." Last night had been a step in the right direction, but she still couldn't say that Troy was the man she wanted to spend the rest of her life with. Olivia hoisted herself onto a tall, wrought-iron stool on the opposite side of the marble-topped counter. “Just because I’m pregnant doesn’t mean we’re meant to be together forever.”

Bianca, who made no pretense of helping with the salad preparation, rested her elbows on the counter and leaned toward her. “How did it happen?”

“Aren’t you a little too old for a lecture on the birds and the bees?”

“I’m serious.” Bianca tapped an aggressive little fingernail on the polished marble. “You’re a careful, smart, methodical woman. I want to know how you ended up having unprotected sex.”

“I didn’t. The condom broke.”

“An easy explanation,” Bianca said. “It’s not enough. According to your statement, you didn’t know Troy well. Yet, you went to bed with him. Is that typical behavior?”

Olivia had the distinct impression that her sister was cross-examining her. “Why are you doing this?”

“You’re my sister, and I care about you. And about my unborn nephew. Something happened that threw you into Troy’s arms, and I want to know what it was.”

Her mother turned toward them. “As do I.”

Two sets of bright blue eyes focused on her. Olivia didn’t want to talk about that night. She hadn't told anyone but Troy about the traumatic events that drove her to his doorstep, desperately seeking warmth and consolation. "It's none of your business."

"Did he hurt you?" her mother asked.

"No."

Her mother circled the counter, perched on the stool beside Olivia and took both her hands. "We've had too many secrets in this family. It's time for us to open up to each other."

She squeezed her mom's hands. Her skin was cool and damp from washing the salad vegetables. Moments ago, Olivia had demanded to be included in a top secret talk with her parents and Troy. Now the spotlight had shifted and she felt the glare of a thousand-watt bulb. *Be careful what you wish for.* She wanted the secrecy to end, and that meant she had to face the hard, painful truth.

"It was November," she said. "The weather in the mountains was snowy, cold and wet. I had been working with a couple, Jarvis and Carol Rainer, for several months, and Carol was almost due."

And now Carol was working at the clinic with Troy's brother. It was hard to imagine. "Jarvis and Carol weren't my typical clients. They're very wealthy. Their house outside Dillon was practically a castle, and they had a gorgeous yacht on the lake. If they wanted special treatment for

Carol's prenatal care and delivery, they had enough money to buy a wing of a hospital."

Bianca asked, "Is money usually a consideration for couples using a midwife?"

"Sometimes. A home birth is certainly less expensive than a hospital stay. But most people who use me are more concerned about having a natural birthing experience. That's what Carol Rainer wanted." Olivia remembered Carol's easy laugh and her sturdy, athletic build. "She was diligent about following the exercises and watching her diet. Her husband wasn't as interested in the process. He's an aggressive businessman who doesn't like anything he can't control."

"I know the type," Bianca said. "I work for them."

"Anyway, I had planned with Carol and Jarvis to meet at St. Agnes Hospital in Summit County when she went into labor. You'd think a powerhouse like Jarvis might insist on the most prestigious ob-gyn in the country, but St. Agnes has a great reputation. It's a relatively new hospital, and the birthing facility is top-notch. Labor suites are spacious and comfy with electric fireplaces and mountain views through the windows. There are a couple of whirlpool baths. And you can order in gourmet food."

Her story was about to turn ugly. She glanced toward the front of the house, hoping that Troy and her dad would come into the kitchen and interrupt.

"And then?" Bianca prompted.

"It was after dark when Jarvis called me to say that Carol was in labor. He sounded angry and hysterical. I tried to reassure him, to convince him that his wife would probably be in labor for hours, but he insisted that she was ready to deliver the baby. Either way, I didn't think he should be driving. I told him I'd call an ambulance to pick them up. Jarvis refused. He didn't want to wait."

The horror of that night was fresh in her mind. She blinked and saw herself running from her cabin to her SUV, parked inside the garage. She threw the backpack with the supplies she needed to help a mother in labor into the rear and got behind the wheel. In the winter cold, her breath fogged the air. When she pulled out, her headlights illuminated the swirling snow crystals.

She continued, "It was the worst kind of weather for driving. Not a heavy snowfall but ice falling from the sky and coating the surface of the road."

Her tires had skidded and slipped on patches of black ice. Rising tension had elevated her pulse rate to a state near panic. "When I got to the main road, I thought it would be better, but it wasn't. The snow plows hadn't come through. I saw the headlights from the Rainers' Hummer. They'd gone off the road."

Inside her head, Olivia heard herself screaming. It was an endless, all-consuming wail that tore from her lungs and assaulted her ears. Much later that night when she'd told Troy about the accident, he'd held her tight. His strength had given her courage. The heat from his body had warmed her blood.

If he hadn't been there for her, she might have collapsed into a depression so deep that she'd never emerge. Troy had been able to understand the depth of her sadness. He'd been in battle. In his deep voice, he'd spoken of troops who were killed in combat. He had shared her sorrow and eased her pain.

"I parked at the scene of the accident. I thought I was going to fall apart, but I didn't."

Her training had kept her together as she leaped from her vehicle. Dragging her backpack with her equipment, she had scrambled through ankle-deep snow to the Hummer that had crashed through a barbed wire fence into a pine tree. "Jarvis ran toward me. He waved his cell phone and shouted something about a helicopter evacuation."

"But you were close to a hospital," Bianca said. "Why not go there?"

"Carol's injuries were pretty bad. Even Jarvis could see that her condition was serious. He wanted the best specialists for her and the baby."

"And your trained medical opinion didn't matter," Bianca concluded. "I'm surprised the Flight for Life chopper would take off in that kind of weather."

"This helicopter belonged to the Rainer Corporation. It was Jarvis's private transport. They had clearance to fly. Keep in mind that the weather in Denver was mild compared to what we were getting in the mountains."

Her mom leaned forward. "What happened next, dear?"

Olivia had thought she'd burst into tears at this point, but her eyes were dry. At some level the trauma was too great and she detached herself, speaking as though these terrible events were someone else's experience. "The impact of the crash must have been huge because the hood of the Hummer was dented, and it takes a lot to damage those beasts. The tires were buried in the wet ground beneath the snow, probably from Jarvis trying to pull away. I wrenched open the passenger side door and saw Carol. I don't think she'd been wearing her seat belt. Her right ankle was broken. She'd whacked her forehead. Blood poured down her face. She was in hard labor. The baby was already crowning."

Olivia had been concerned about possible internal injuries to mother and child. Delivering the baby had been the only choice. She'd tried to get Carol to listen to her, but the woman had been unable to focus. Her body was determined to push. In moments, the tiny baby boy had slipped into Olivia's waiting hands. "He wasn't breathing. The baby wasn't breathing."

She had a few minutes before the situation became serious. As long as the placenta was attached, the newborn would receive oxygenated blood through the umbilical cord. Using her finger, she had cleared the baby's mouth. She had placed him on his mother's stomach and rubbed hard along his backbone to stimulate breathing.

"Carol lost consciousness. She was hemorrhaging."

"And the baby?" Bianca asked.

"Still not breathing. I don't know how I managed to get the bag and mask from my backpack, but I did. I got him ventilated. That should have taken care of the problem."

But nothing she had done had any effect. Twice before, she'd been in situations where the newborn was slow to draw a first breath, but those times had been in a hospital with a whole team working to save the baby. Once they'd succeeded. The second time was a failure.

She tried infant CPR, covering his nose and mouth and exhaling shallow breaths into his body.

She'd pressed on his chest between his nipples to encourage his lungs.

"He was turning blue."

The logical portion of her brain told her that the baby had been fatally injured while he was still inside his mother's womb, but her heart wouldn't let her give up hope. She kept working on the tiny body.

Carol's body convulsed as she expelled the placenta. There was so much blood.

"Jarvis and his men got Carol, me and the baby into the chopper. It was so loud. And so cold."

She'd unzipped her parka and held the cold, lifeless baby against her chest, trying to infuse him with warmth. The seconds ticked away. Every passing minute lessened his chance for survival.

"I did everything I could. But it wasn't enough. When the chopper got to the hospital, they pried the baby out of my arms."

Her mother left her stool and embraced her daughter. "I'm so sorry you had to go through that."

"Jarvis was yelling at me, telling me that it was all my fault."

"But it wasn't," Bianca said.

"How can you be so sure?"

"Someone like Jarvis would have insisted on

an investigation. If he had any basis to sue you for malpractice, he would have."

Later, Olivia had learned that the baby had sustained head and spinal injuries during the accident. He was born dead.

Carol's condition had been critical, but she'd survived. And she was a changed woman—working at the homeless clinic and separated from Jarvis.

"I felt like it was my fault." Olivia gave her mother a squeeze and looked into her eyes. "I don't think I'll ever make peace with what happened. But I've learned to live with the sadness, and I'm grateful—so grateful—for every successful birthing I attend."

Her mom stroked her cheek. "I'm glad you told us."

So was Olivia. She felt supported and safe in the arms of her family. Never before had she burdened them with her personal problems, never before had she shared.

"How did Troy get involved?" Bianca asked.

"After I left the hospital, I just wandered up and down the streets. I didn't really have a destination but I looked up and saw that I was outside Troy's brother's house."

"Wait a sec," Bianca said. "Were you dating the brother?"

"No, we're just friends. I come into town once

or twice a month to volunteer at the homeless clinic, remember?"

"Sure." Bianca nodded. "You usually stay with me."

"Troy's brother, Alex, works at the clinic, too."

"I'm liking this guy more and more," Bianca said. "After you realized you were outside Alex's house, then what?"

"I knew if I talked to Alex, he'd say all the right things to comfort me. But that wasn't what I was looking for. I wanted to see Troy."

"Does he live with his brother?"

"Most of his work is overseas or at Camp Lejeune. When he's in Denver, he stays with his brother. Alex had fixed us up, and we'd been on two casual dates. We definitely didn't have a relationship."

"And yet, you went looking for him," Bianca said. "Why?"

A very good question. She'd thought about it dozens of times. Had fate driven her toward Troy? In her subconscious mind, had she known that he was supposed to be the father of her child? She didn't have an answer.

"After the accident, I wasn't thinking in my right mind. Nothing made sense. All I wanted was to make love. I wanted the heat of passion to melt the cold, dead horror I felt inside. Troy was the perfect candidate. I could have wild, life-affirming sex with him and would probably never see him again."

Olivia glanced toward her mom. This wasn't the kind of topic they usually discussed. All kinds of secrets were being explored today.

"I understand," her mother said.

Bianca blinked in surprise. "You do?"

"As you girls have long suspected, your father and I are involved in a profession that involves a certain amount of danger. I've seen my share of tragedy. I know the pain of losing a friend or an associate. It helps to be able to rekindle your spirit in passion."

Her aristocratic, champagne-blonde mother in her smooth, beige pants outfit certainly didn't look like the sort of woman who would be swept up in a wild, hot-blooded fervor. But she also didn't seem like the type to be wearing an ankle holster.

Bianca glanced back and forth between both of them. "I'll say it again. Wow."

Chapter Nine

The GPS locator planted among Olivia's things was proving difficult to find, even with a bug sweeper. Troy was glad. If Olivia's dad had uncovered the device in a few moments, he would have felt like a complete fool.

They had unloaded the Range Rover and carried the luggage upstairs to the second guest bedroom. The two twin beds and flowered curtains made Troy nostalgic for the classy suite they'd stayed in last night. He watched as Richard used his electronic sweeper to go over Olivia's huge suitcase for the third time. Finding nothing, he muttered, "Are you certain there's a locator?"

"It's the only way they could have picked up our trail on the highway."

"They weren't simply using her cell phone?"

"I disabled the GPS on her phone. My cell is encrypted and secure." He circled the pile of luggage. "There's still her purse, the backpack with her birthing equipment and her laptop."

"Apparently, my daughter finds it necessary to travel with all her earthly belongings." When he picked up the scruffy-looking backpack, her equipment rattled around like a toolbox. "What's in here?"

"Stethoscope, fetal monitor, medical stuff." Troy had already checked the assortment. "Also sheets, latex gloves, scrubs and a couple of teddy bears."

Richard carefully felt along the seams. "When you first told me that someone was trying to kidnap Olivia, I found it difficult to believe."

"Initially, I had the same reaction. Being chased down the highway from the mountains by two vehicles convinced me."

"You never said how you extricated yourself."

"We had a police escort into town."

While he described Olivia's faked labor and equally fake triplets, her dad listened with an expression of concern and amusement. "She did that? My sweet little Olivia lied to a police officer?"

"That's right."

Richard smoothed his white hair. "I'm proud of her for thinking fast. At the same time, it scares the hell out of me."

"I know what you mean."

"When I look at Olivia, I still see a little girl with a messy ponytail and freckles and scraped knees. She was a blur, always running from one thing to another with no consideration for her personal safety."

Her fierce, energetic, adventurous spirit was how she'd gotten kidnapped as a child. According to her story, she'd thrown herself into the clutches of the kidnappers. "Protecting her isn't going to be easy."

"I'd like to lock her up in a bulletproof case. Being a father is the most difficult and dangerous mission I've ever undertaken."

"Dangerous?"

"I'm quite sure you know what I mean." When Richard focused, he had a ferocious intensity. In spite of the blazer with gold buttons and the polished loafers, he was a man of action. "A threat to someone you love is far more dangerous and terrifying than a bullet whizzing toward the center of your forehead."

Troy acknowledged his logic with a quick nod. "You've done a good job with your girls. They're both independent and strong."

"Perhaps too much so."

In her computer case, Richard found the GPS locator tucked into a corner. He removed the small device and studied it. "Standard issue. Nothing unusual about this equipment. It could belong to anyone."

"It's further proof of the threat." Troy sat on

the edge of one of the twin beds. "Before we go downstairs and join the women, we should come up with a plan of action."

"Glad you think so." Richard sat on the other bed, facing him. He crossed his legs and straightened the sharp crease in his trousers. "When you insisted that we share information, I feared that you were open to a free-for-all discussion."

"I told Olivia that I'd keep her informed and listen to her opinion. But the decision when it comes to her safety is mine. You and I are the professionals. We decide what's best."

"And my wife," he said. "To be quite honest, she's probably a better spy than I am. Speaks seven languages fluently. And she remembers everything. She started with the CIA as an information analyst, but she's not the sort of woman who is content with a desk job."

"Much like her daughters." Getting these women to agree to protective custody wouldn't be easy. "I've analyzed the nature of the threat, and here's what I'm thinking. The end goal isn't to physically harm Olivia."

Richard asked, "What's your basis for that conclusion?"

"She said that she had the sense of being followed for several days. If someone had wanted her dead, they had plenty of opportunity. Even when we were being chased, it wasn't a hard-core pursuit. The vehicles hung back. They weren't trying to kill us."

"How very reassuring."

"That's why I'm finding it hard to believe that the Hatari terrorists are involved. These guys are violent. They've lived through bloody massacres in their homeland. They think nothing of wiping out an entire village in Rwanda. They aren't clever or subtle."

"On the other hand, Kruger is known for his adept evasion of discovery," Richard said. "But I can't imagine why he'd focus on me. He's not my nemesis. I haven't heard his name in years."

"Maybe you have," Troy said. "His alias could have changed."

"We need more information."

"There's a problem of jurisdiction," Troy reminded him. "My marines don't have authority inside the United States. Our information comes through the navy's criminal investigators and homeland security."

"Likewise for the CIA." Richard stood. "I suggest that you contact your point man for an update, and we'll join the ladies for lunch. We will inform them—all three of them—that they need to stay here at Bianca's house."

"For their own safety," Troy said.

"Surely, they'll understand."

"I wouldn't bet on it."

"NOT A CHANCE," Bianca said as she pushed her chair back from the dining table. "I can't stay locked up in my house. I have a job."

"Take a few days off," Dad said as he returned from the kitchen. "I'm sure your law firm will survive."

"It's not about them. It's about me. I'm on track to make partner," Bianca said. "There's an important dinner I need to attend tonight. *We* need to attend. Remember, Dad?"

"Yes, of course."

Olivia could tell by his guarded expression that her father had completely spaced out the formal dinner that was apparently important to her sister's career. After her heart-to-heart talk with her mom and Bianca, she felt like the balance of family relationships was in chaos. The polite civility that marked most of their luncheons had been replaced by a reckless urge to blurt out the truth. And the chardonnay was flowing.

She wasn't drinking, and Troy had left the table to take a phone call, but the other three Laughtons had already polished off one bottle of French wine with their quiche. Standing at the head of the table, her dad pulled the cork from a second bottle. As he poured a healthy dose into Sharon's wineglass, he said, "Try to understand, Bianca. I'm trying to protect you."

"I'll stay home this afternoon," Bianca said, "but I'm going to that dinner."

Olivia asked, "What's so important about this dinner?"

"It's a reception for a Saudi prince and his entourage. One of our biggest clients, CRG Energy Group, is trying to solidify a deal with him. I met the prince once before, and he specifically asked for me to be there."

"Maybe you can be wife number three," Olivia teased.

"Very funny. He's not married."

"And quite a handsome young man," Mom said. "Amir was educated at Oxford, and he plays the violin. Your father and I met him at a recital that featured Yo-Yo Ma."

"Yo-Yo Ma?" Olivia was impressed. "Really?"

"It's my cover, dear. Cultural affairs at various embassies." She smiled fondly at her husband. "We've led a very interesting life."

"Amir remembers them," Bianca said. "That's why he wanted them to be invited to the reception."

"Do you think we can arrange for Olivia and Troy to come?" Mom asked.

Olivia wasn't thrilled with that idea. She'd rather have private time with Troy. "We'll skip."

"This is more than a social occasion." Mom delicately sipped her chardonnay. "According to our sources, Kruger is involved with the oil business. This dinner might connect to our investigation."

"Investigation?" Her dad lowered himself into his chair. "We're not investigating."

"We should be," Mom said brightly. "The best way to eliminate a threat is to find the source."

Olivia wondered how often the gourmet dinner parties that her parents arranged were covers for investigations or opportunities to gather intelligence. Being spies meant they were constantly on the lookout, constantly under threat. The fact that she and her sister had managed to sneak out of the house for late-night parties was kind of amazing.

"Here's an idea," Bianca said. "Why don't we call the police?"

"Oh, my dear." Mom looked down her nose with none-too-subtle disparagement. "This is much more than a simple police action. The CIA and various homeland security agencies are involved. I would imagine that Troy has also been in contact with military intelligence and NCIS."

"Why?"

"It has something to do with a sleeper spy named Kruger that your father and I might or might not have known." She raised her wineglass toward her husband, and they clinked rims. "I must say, I'm enjoying this new atmosphere of truth-telling. We should have done this years ago."

Bianca stared across the table at Olivia. "Make it stop."

"Too late," Olivia muttered.

Her sophisticated parents—Mr. and Mrs. Super Spy—were obviously enjoying themselves. They had so much in common. Shared occupation. Shared interest in the arts. Shared love of world travel. Both slim and elegant, they looked like they belonged together.

When Olivia spotted Troy sauntering down the hallway toward the table, she knew they'd never be a perfect match like her parents. He was a marine, first and foremost. His training directed him toward quick, aggressive action. Her career was all about patience and nurturing. They'd grown up in different worlds, experienced different things.

He straightened his shoulders before entering the room. His chin lifted, and his easygoing manner was replaced by determination. She recognized his attitude in the tensing of his muscles, and she knew he was preparing for battle. Neither she nor her family was the enemy, but they were all strong personalities. Dealing with the Laughtons was difficult, and she admired him for taking on the challenge.

He never gave up. How many times had he proposed marriage? At least a dozen. Any other man would have turned his back and walked away. Not Troy. When he set a goal, he was relentless.

Her hand rested on her belly. Until last night, she'd thought his only concern was the baby and his responsibilities as a father. The way he'd held her and touched her made her think otherwise. He was after her, as well. He wanted her.

And she enjoyed being the object of his pursuit. Seeing him was a pleasure. Looking at his gorgeous body and handsome face made her heart jump. Physically, he was everything she wanted in a man. If he turned away from her now, she might reverse course and start going after him.

Unlike her parents, she and Troy weren't birds of a feather. They were an unlikely couple, but their bond grew stronger every moment they were together.

The atmosphere around the table changed when he returned to his seat beside her. His bearing was serious, but his voice was matter-of-fact and calm. "I've just gotten off the phone with Gunnery Sergeant Nelson. He's my point man on the Hatari terrorist cell, and he's coordinating intelligence with several other agencies."

"Including ours?" her mother asked.

"Yes, ma'am. CIA is front and center. They have the most intelligence on Kruger, who they suspect of involvement in financing arms deals through Africa."

"Recently?"

"Yes, ma'am."

"That's how he might have come into contact with Hatari," her father said. "Has Kruger been identified?"

"He's still under deep cover." Troy took out his cell phone, tapped a few buttons and pulled up a photo. "The best they could do were three photographs from twenty-two years ago when Kruger first entered the United States."

"Three pictures of different men?" Olivia asked.

"I'll explain," her father said. "Kruger was supposed to meet with a Mossad agent who was under surveillance. The agent had contact with three different men. These photos were taken with a long-range lens on city streets, and they're terribly blurred. None of the men could be identified."

"Wait a minute," Bianca said. "Mossad is the Israeli secret service. Doesn't that mean they're on our side?"

Quietly, Troy said, "Those lines got blurred. The Mossad agent was killed before he could be taken into custody and debriefed."

"A botched mission," her father said. "Kruger went his merry way to establish his deep cover identity. We can assume his appearance was altered. His fingerprints were never on file."

Olivia couldn't believe they were talking about these things. Sitting around the lunch table with the remains of quiche and a bottle of chardonnay, her family was calmly chatting about spy missions, assassinations and Mossad agents. Who were these people? And what had they done with her ultrasecretive parents?

Troy handed the cell phone with the photos to her father. "I'd appreciate if you take a look."

"A waste of time," he said dismissively. "I've seen these pictures before."

"With all due respect," Troy said, "technology has improved in the past twenty-two years. These photos have been digitally enhanced."

"I haven't seen them," Mom said as she held out her hand for the phone. "Richard, darling, why was I kept in the dark?"

"Twenty-two years ago," her father said, "you weren't working in the field."

Olivia knew exactly what had happened twenty-two years ago. It was after she and her mom had been kidnapped, and the family moved to Washington, D.C., where they settled down until both daughters were through high school. Was it possible that Kruger and the current kidnapping attempt were related to what had happened so long ago?

As her mother scanned the photos, Olivia watched her expression. When she was a child, she'd been able to read every nuance of her mother's moods. As she grew up, they had lost that connection.

When her mom looked up from the cell phone and met her gaze, Olivia saw a flash of anger. "What is it, Mom?"

"I know this man."

Chapter Ten

Troy reached over and took Olivia's hand. She had gasped when her mother had made her announcement, and his natural instinct was to protect the mother of his unborn son. From what? Her own mother? Troy had the uneasy feeling that Olivia's family could hurt her more than any other perceived threat.

He shot a quick glance in her direction. Her face showed a mirror reflection of her mother's tension. Damn it, this wasn't the way things should be. A pregnant lady should be surrounded by tranquility and peace with somebody massaging her feet and somebody else feeding her grapes. She needed serenity. Not spy chasing.

And he was as guilty as the rest of them. He'd taken her condition for granted and assumed that she could handle everything herself. That attitude had to change.

Looking toward Sharon Laughton, Troy asked, "Ma'am, are you sure about the identification?"

"I know him," she said firmly.

"Did you meet Kruger years ago?"

"No, I don't believe I did."

Troy wasn't following her comments. "Are you saying that you've met him recently?"

She nodded. "He looks different now. There are typical changes due to aging, like his receding hairline. I'd guess that at some time he had plastic surgery to modify his nose and the line of his jaw. Still, the resemblance is blatantly obvious. It's the shape of his ears. Ears don't change. They're unique to each individual and are an excellent means of identification."

Her husband left his chair, circled the table and stood behind her. When he checked out the photo on the cell phone, his eyebrows raised. "She's right."

"You bet I am."

Olivia's mother had transformed from a beige sophisticate into a tiger mom. Her cheeks flushed. Her lips drew back in a snarl that revealed perfect white teeth. "What level of incompetence would allow this individual to go undetected? I cannot abide this nonsense. Not when it endangers my children."

"Again, she's right." Richard backed her up. "Kruger must be taken into custody immediately."

Troy wasn't sure what the hell they were talking about. He was missing something. "Let me get this straight. You both know this man?"

"Yes," they said in chorus.

Through a clenched jaw, he asked, "Can you give me a name?"

Olivia's mother passed the cell phone to Bianca. "Why don't you do the honors, dear? Tell him."

Bianca stared blankly at the screen. "I don't see it."

"The ears," her mother said. "Look at his ears."

"Still not getting it," Bianca said.

"Really, darling. Imagine this young man with twenty years of hard living. His hair is steel-gray. His forehead is creased, and he has deep lines at the edge of his mouth."

"Sorry, Mom," Bianca snapped. "I haven't had your training. I haven't spent my whole life studying faces and being paranoid. I deal with facts. Not innuendo."

"And I'm proud of you," her mother said. "I'm proud of both my daughters."

Troy heard Olivia draw a ragged breath. She was on the verge of hormonal tears again, and he didn't want to go through another bout of emotion. "We've had enough guessing games. I need a name."

"Matthew Clark," Richard said. "He's one of

the principals in CRG Energy. They're clients of Bianca's law firm."

Bianca stared at the photo, blinked and looked up. In a small voice, she said, "It's him."

Other information Troy had received suggested that Kruger was involved in the oil business. "Earlier, when I talked with Sergeant Nelson, he mentioned that they'd picked up chatter about Denver. I never thought the connection would be so close."

"What happens now?" Olivia asked.

The others talked at once. Bianca wanted the bastard to be arrested and subjected to a humiliating perp walk. Richard insisted upon informing his superiors at the CIA while Sharon sneered at the CIA for not locating Kruger sooner and suggested that they personally take him into custody and find out what he knew.

"Enough." Troy rose to his feet. "This is my operation. Apprehending Kruger is not our prime objective. We've got a terrorist cell planning to blow up a building in Manhattan. They need to be stopped."

"Of course," Olivia's mother said as she sipped her chardonnay. "You need to check with your people, Troy. In the meantime, we should all get ready for the dinner tonight. Bianca, please arrange for Olivia and Troy to be guests. Olivia, do you have anything appropriate to wear?"

"I do."

"Excellent. For dinner tonight, you and Troy will pretend to be engaged. It simplifies introductions if we can say he's your fiancé."

Olivia started to object, "I'm not going to—"

"You need a nap," her mother said as she rose from the table. "It's already been a long day, and we'll be out late tonight."

Troy was pretty sure that his authority had been usurped and he'd been managed by the elegant hand of Sharon Laughton. She was damn good at what she did.

IN THE GUEST bedroom, Olivia lay on her side on the bed closest to the window and stared at the afternoon light that spilled around the edge of the flowered curtain. Seeing her parents acting like CIA operatives wasn't really a shock. At some level, she and Bianca had always known that Mom and Dad were more than diplomats who traveled the globe.

But their behavior was strange. Her mom wore an ankle holster as an accessory. She recognized other spies by the shape of their ears.

Absentmindedly, she massaged her belly. How was she going to tell her son? Could she really say something like, "Granny and Grandpa are going to be late for your soccer game because they're doing espionage in Uzbekistan"? Explaining Troy's occupation was easier. He was a marine; his job revolved around danger. But Granny and Grandpa? No way could she explain their profession to a child.

Similar to her own childhood, there would be a curtain drawn over a large part of her parents' lives. Was the family secrecy all that important to their relationship with her son? Love should be all that mattered. When she was growing up, Olivia had never felt unloved. Sure, she'd had issues. She'd feared that she'd never measure up to her parents' high expectations and had struggled for their approval. But she had known that her mom and dad loved her.

She heard the bedroom door open and turned her head to see Troy entering on tiptoe.

"You're not disturbing me," she assured him. "I wasn't napping."

He came around the bed and went down on one knee in front of her so he could look her in the eye. "I'd join you on the bed, but I don't think both of us will fit."

"Twin beds," she muttered. Her sister's guest bedroom was perfectly acceptable but it was far from a love nest. "What's the update?"

"According to the CIA and to my people as well, your mother's identification of Matthew Clark as Kruger has an eighty percent chance of being accurate. They're sorting through documents and doing forensic computer searches on Matthew Clark's finances to make sure. But it seems likely."

"Mom must be thrilled."

"She's kind of amazing," he said. "She's angry enough to rip somebody's face off, but she's one hundred percent smooth when she talks to her superiors. Velvet and steel."

An apt description. "Imagine growing up with that."

"I'm guessing that you and Bianca didn't get away with much."

"The odd thing is that we did. Both Mom and Dad trusted us and let us make our own mistakes." She thought back to a couple of teenage catastrophes. "The steely part came when we got caught. Mom never raised her voice, but she could skin us alive with a look."

"My instructions are to proceed as though nothing is different, and we haven't identified Kruger." He gave a shrug. "That means we have to show up for this dinner tonight."

She groaned. "Really?"

"I'm not happy about it, either. My instincts are telling me that something isn't right. I don't know what. Something."

"Lucky for us, I've got something fancy to wear. It's a draping toga thing. Bianca can probably help me out with jewelry."

"So can I." He reached into his pocket. "I've been carrying this around for a while."

Resting on the palm of his hand was a small, black velvet box. She suddenly realized that he was on one knee. Pulling her legs down, she sat on the edge of the bed. "This doesn't mean we're engaged. Not for real."

"Got it," he said. "But your mom was right. It's easier to explain our relationship by saying we're engaged."

He flipped open the lid to the box and showed her a square-cut diamond solitaire with a white platinum band. Even though they weren't really getting engaged, her heart fluttered. The brilliance of the stone took her breath away. "It's beautiful."

"I'm glad you'll be wearing the ring. Even if it's only for tonight."

When he slipped it onto her finger, she held up her hand to admire the sparkle. For a moment, she allowed herself to sink into a wedding fantasy, imagining herself in a stunning white gown and a veil. Her bouquet would be white orchids. She'd walk down the aisle with her handsome father and Troy would be waiting in his tuxedo—no, in his marine dress blues. And he'd look like a hero, her special hero. She could almost hear the organ music in the background.

When she gazed down at him, she wanted

to accept this ring for what it really meant. She wanted to be engaged to him.

Still on one knee, he met her gaze. "The ring looks good on you."

"It's kind of tight," she said. "My fingers are swollen."

"Because of this little guy." He rested his hands on either side of her belly, leaned forward and placed a kiss at the place where her waist should be. Then he stood and kissed her forehead.

Though she didn't think his kisses were meant to send a message, she drew her own conclusion: the baby came first.

If she hadn't been pregnant, Troy never would have asked her to marry him. Their relationship was only about the baby. He'd never told her that he loved her. There was no basis for a wedding, much less a marriage.

"There are a couple things I want to talk to you about," he said. "Are you up for a talk or would you rather nap?"

"I'll lie down," she said, sinking into an unreasonable state of gloom as she stretched out on the bed. If she hadn't been carrying his child, he wouldn't even be here.

"I'll join you."

"The bed is too skinny."

"Not a problem."

Quickly, Troy reconfigured the room, shoving

the twin beds together. He kicked off his shoes and lay on the bed beside her, within easy reach. His hand stroked from her shoulder to her belly and back again.

The sensual warmth that came every time they were physically close immediately lifted her spirits. Though he didn't love her, they were lovers. Their sexual chemistry might not be a sufficient basis for marriage, but it was pretty remarkable.

His long leg wrapped around her thigh, and he pulled her closer. The sensation of his body pressed against hers was becoming more and more familiar. They fit together well.

"What did you want to talk about?" she asked.

"When I put everything together, it doesn't make sense. Let's say that Matthew Clark really is Kruger, the mysterious spy. Why would he want to kidnap you?"

"To get to my parents," she suggested.

"Why you? It's more logical for him to go after Bianca. He already knows her."

She watched his mouth as he spoke. His lower lip was fuller than the upper, and the corners turned up. Would their child look like him?

"Olivia?" He called her back to the topic.

"I'm listening," she said quickly. "What did your sources tell you about the kidnap attempt?"

"The tactic sounds like Kruger, but there's no indication that he knows your parents. They only met once. It was last winter at a CRG Energy Christmas party."

With the tip of her finger, she traced his lips. "When Bianca and I introduce our parents, we usually say something vague, like they work for the State Department. Maybe Kruger got curious about them, did research and found out that they were CIA."

"Their identities are buried," he said. "I had to call in a bunch of favors and use my top secret security clearance to get information on your parents."

She was far more interested in the shape of his lips and jaw than in speculating about spies. "Maybe the connection is to you. Not my parents. The kidnapping could be part of the Hatari scheme."

"It's possible."

She vividly remembered his characterization of the Hatari cell as vicious killers. "What else could it be?"

"There might be a more personal reason for someone to kidnap you." He laced his fingers through hers. When her hand turned, the diamond caught the light and shimmered. "There could be someone with a grudge."

"Against me?"

"A jealous ex-boyfriend. Or a stalker? Or somebody you offended?"

"Oh, puh-leeze. I'm a midwife. I don't have nefarious enemies lurking around every corner."

"Everybody has enemies. Even you."

"Nope, I'm perfect."

She leaned forward to kiss him but he pulled back.

"Nobody's perfect," he said. "My brother is one of the most decent men I've ever known, and he has enemies. There was a guy he treated at the clinic who got ticked off and came after Alex with a gun."

"I heard about that."

"I hate to bring this up. When we saw Alex at the hospital, he mentioned Carol Rainer."

Olivia shoved away from him and rolled onto her back. She didn't like to think about the Rainers and what happened on that cold night last November. Carol might blame her for the loss of her baby. "I was wrong. There are people who hate me."

"We should probably talk to Carol."

Even if Carol Rainer despised her down to her toes, Olivia found it difficult to imagine the outdoorsy woman from Dillon involved in a two-car chase through the foothills. "If this is your idea of foreplay, you might want to rethink your technique."

He bridged the gap between the beds. With an impressive show of strength, he flipped her toward him and adjusted her body so she was facing him. His kiss was long, slow and deep.

She forgot about everything else.

Chapter Eleven

The party for Bianca's law firm to welcome the Saudi prince and the higher-up executives from CRG Energy Group took place at a private home in an old-money neighborhood with winding streets. It wasn't the sort of home Olivia ever aspired to own. She liked to keep things simple, and this place was definitely high-maintenance. Three stories with five chimney stacks, the house sprawled across an acre of prime Denver real estate.

In the early evening dusk, garden spotlights illuminated the yard. As Troy drove their Range Rover into a line of cars proceeding around the circular drive, she peered through the windshield. "How many gardeners do you think it takes to keep the grounds looking so lush and gorgeous? All the flowers are blooming. The grass is perfect."

"It's nice," Troy said.

"'Nice' doesn't begin to describe it." She pointed

to a grouping of dwarf apple trees with fruit hanging from the boughs. "There's proof. This garden is Eden."

"Does that make us Adam and Eve?"

"And Kruger is the snake in the grass."

"When you meet him—"

"I know," she interrupted. "I'm not supposed to mouth off. Mom told me to smile and look innocent."

"You're not the one I'm worried about."

"Then who? Surely not my parents."

"Bianca's got her feathers ruffled. She's seeing Matthew Clark's undercover identity as a personal betrayal." A muscle in his jaw tensed. "Bianca needs to be cautious."

He'd been on edge since his last conversation with Sergeant Nelson. On the way to his brother's house to borrow a suit, Troy had barely said a word.

She reached over and touched his forearm. "What's wrong?"

"I don't like the way this is playing out. There are too many people involved, too many different agencies. Somebody is going to drop the ball."

"Maybe we'll get lucky and Kruger won't be here."

"He'd better show," he said. "A forensic team is going to be searching his condo while he's here."

"Is that legal? Don't they need warrants?"

"We're talking about CIA and homeland security."

She knew what was wrong. "You don't like this because you're not in charge."

"I wouldn't mind if I knew who was actually giving the orders." He craned his neck to see around the line of cars. "Using the valet doesn't work for me. We might need to make a quick escape."

He cranked the steering wheel and exited the line of cars. Opposite the front door, their Range Rover was stopped by a teenager in a valet vest.

Troy lowered the driver's side window. "I'd rather park it myself."

"Sorry, sir," the valet said. "We're supposed to take care of all the vehicles."

"I have a special circumstance." Troy jabbed a thumb in her direction. "My fiancée is nine months pregnant. We might need to leave in a hurry."

The kid in the red vest stared through the window at her belly. He swallowed repeatedly, causing his Adam's apple to bounce up and down like a yo-yo. "You can park on the side by the catering trucks."

"And I'll hang on to my car keys." Troy turned to her. "Should I let you out here?"

"Yes, please." Though she was fully capable of walking, her sister had talked her into wearing high heels that made every step precarious. "I'll see you inside."

She stepped across the flagstones at the entryway and entered through double doors that were opened wide. Watching these attractive people in designer cocktail dresses and suits reminded her of the soirees and galas she'd attended while growing up as the daughter of Washington, D.C., diplomats. Her mother's connections in the art world got them invited to tons of cultural events. Her parents knew everybody, and people loved to have the supercharming Laughtons in attendance.

Moving stiffly in her heels, she made her way into a vast room with an inlaid parquet floor. There must have been over two hundred people there, but the house didn't seem crowded. French doors opened onto an outdoor patio where small groups had gathered. There were three buffet stations, several bars and circulating waiters in white shirts and black bow ties. A gentle undercurrent of music came from the grand piano in a library-type room.

She spotted her parents. They blended perfectly into this crowd. Her white-haired father was dignified, and her mom was sheer elegance in a slim column of peach-colored silk. The skirt was too short for her ankle holster, and Olivia wondered where Mom had hidden her weapon. They were chatting with one of the senior partners in Bianca's law firm, a man Olivia had met but couldn't recall his name. A lapse of memory like that would never be tolerated in a spy. Apparently, she hadn't inherited her parents' ability for espionage.

Bianca stood beside them, shifting her feet and looking nervous. Troy was right to think she might be the loose cannon. Her sister seemed to be laughing too loud and drinking too freely. Would she be the one to drop the ball?

Olivia turned and found herself face-to-face with the chiseled cheekbones and dark eyes of an extremely handsome Saudi man. He introduced himself.

"Prince Amir," she said as she inclined her head. "My name is Olivia. I'm Bianca Laughton's sister."

"I see the resemblance," he said. "You are both quite stunning women."

"Thank you." Her lavender gown with the deep vee neckline draped elegantly over her baby bump. The swirling yards of fabric made her feel beautiful, even sexy. A high slit on the right side showed off her legs and the perilous high heel shoes.

"I've had the pleasure of meeting your mother and father," he said. "Your mother helped coordinate a modern art exhibit in my country."

She had to wonder why Amir had singled her out. When it came to status, she had to be the least important person in attendance at this event. Was there another motive? Olivia didn't have the subtlety of her parents. The only way she knew to get at the truth was to ask directly.

Before she could blurt out an inappropriate question about kidnapping and terrorists, she saw Troy coming toward them, and she was totally distracted. The charcoal suit his brother had loaned him fit perfectly across the wide span of his shoulders. He'd opted not to wear a necktie, and the collar of his light blue shirt set off his tanned complexion. She loved to watch him move. Striding toward her, he was smooth and confident. An intriguing balance of masculinity and sophistication, he looked like he belonged here.

Proudly, she said, "I'd like to introduce my fiancé."

The word rolled easily off her tongue. *Fiancé. Betrothed. The man I will one day marry.* She hadn't expected to make that claim or to have it feel so good.

As if Troy couldn't get any cooler, he greeted Amir in his native language. They exchanged comments and a laugh. And she felt the aura of tension fade away. She wasn't a spy and didn't have to act like one. If Amir was up to something, she'd leave it to Troy to figure out the angles.

Her parents and Bianca joined them and the

prince. Her mother responded to Amir in Arabic—one of the seven languages she spoke fluently. With Mom and Troy and the prince enjoying each other's company, her dad leaned close and whispered, "I saw you come in alone. Where was Troy?"

"He parked the car so we can leave quickly if we need to."

"Avoiding the valet," her dad said. "Smart move."

Though he was talking to her, Olivia realized that her dad's gaze was riveted to her sister. Bianca stood at the fringe of the Arabic conversation with Troy, her mom and the prince. The indecisive expression on her sister's face reminded Olivia of someone on the edge of a cold swimming pool deciding whether or not to jump.

"We are being rude," the prince said as he turned and focused on Bianca. "We should speak English so these lovely ladies can add their opinions."

When her sister smiled back at him, Olivia noticed the spark between them. They were an unlikely couple whose professional relationship would make any personal connection difficult, but their chemistry was obvious. No wonder Bianca was nervous.

From across the room, Olivia felt someone watching her. She scanned the faces of the crowd; no one seemed to be staring in her direction. In any other situation, she would have dismissed this prickly sensation, but it wouldn't go away. She was reminded of how she'd felt outside the hospital in Dillon. *Someone watching. Waiting to make their move.* This wasn't her imagination.

She should have been better prepared, should have listened more carefully when her parents and Troy talked about Kruger. Olivia had seen the fuzzy photograph from long ago, but she didn't know what Matthew Clark looked like.

A man with shaggy, steel-gray hair wearing a beige suit and yellow necktie caught her gaze. Was he Matthew Clark? She gave him a polite smile and a nod. Instead of responding, he looked away. Was this man the focus of the investigation? Was he aware that a forensic team was searching his condo at this very moment? Did he feel the danger?

Her father nudged her shoulder. "Don't stare."

Though she wanted to ask if that man was Matthew Clark, she had no desire to be more deeply involved in espionage. *This is not my job.* She linked arms with Troy. "At the risk of sounding like a cliché of a pregnant woman," she said, "I'm starving. Can we hit the buffet?"

"Thought you'd never ask," he said.

As they crossed the room, she whispered, "The guy in the yellow necktie has been watching me."

"That's Clark."

A knot of fear tightened inside her chest. Her heart skipped. "Should I be worried?"

"I'll take care of you," he promised. "Stay close to me. I'll keep you safe."

She trusted that he would.

TROY WASN'T CUT out for this type of espionage. He was uncomfortable at large social gatherings where every comment twisted into double and triple meanings. Allegiances shifted as easily as the direction of the wind. No one could be trusted. His type of intelligence mission was to go forward with a clear objective, with guns blazing if necessary.

His assignment at this party was supposed to be simple. When Matthew Clark left, Troy would send a text message to the team that was searching Clark's condo. His message would be their signal to get the hell out.

It should have been simple. But Troy had reasons for concern. For one thing, Clark appeared unduly nervous. His behavior was furtive, as though he knew he'd been identified.

Earlier, while Troy was parking their vehicle near the service entrance, he had noticed one delivery van that was unlike the others. The logo for a cake baker on the side of that van had been applied in a rush, which made Troy wonder if somebody had used that van to get inside the house.

There was virtually no security at this event. With the exception of the prince's entourage—three of those guys were armed—there were no bodyguards. Nor had the guests been checked off an approved list. Dozens of anonymous waiters, waitresses and bartenders were circulating. All of them wore white shirts and black bowties, a simple disguise.

Troy's gut told him that Kruger, alias Matthew Clark, was in danger. After twenty-two years undercover, he must have been involved in a lot of nefarious plots. He had to know secrets that others would kill for, which would explain his nerves.

Though Troy had passed on his observations to Nelson, he'd heard nothing back. His apprehension heightened as he observed Olivia's CIA parents and her obviously frazzled sister milling through the room.

Beside him, Olivia downed another pastry puff and sighed. "This food is delicious. Have you tried the crab cakes?"

"How could I? You cleaned the platter."

"The waiter said he'd bring more." She looked through the crowd. "He's over there by the fireplace. You think he's avoiding me?"

Looking down at her, he couldn't help smiling. In her purple dress with her long, blond hair curling around her face, she was beautiful in a different way than usual. She was elegant. And he liked the way his ring shimmered on her finger.

Maybe he was overreacting to the Clark situation. Maybe she'd been right when she'd said the real problem was that he hated any situation where he wasn't in control.

"Should we go after the waiter with the crab cakes?" he asked.

"Let's track him down."

Their path was blocked by Matthew Clark. For a man who'd had extensive reconstructive surgery on his face, he looked natural. Clark had avoided the temptation to change himself into the sexiest man alive. His appearance was average, nondescript. His shaggy, gray hair mostly covered his ears, which made Troy wonder how Olivia's mother had gotten a close enough look to identify him.

Clark introduced himself to Olivia. "I've been watching you," he admitted. "You're Bianca's sister, right?"

"Right." She gestured with her plate. "I would shake hands, but I'm kind of occupied."

"Have we met before?" he asked.

"I don't think so."

She introduced Troy, who shook hands and realized immediately that Clark had no special interest in him, which seemed strange. Even if Clark hadn't made the connection to Hatari, he had to know that Troy had been driving the car that his men had chased into town.

Clark turned back toward Olivia. “I seem to remember meeting your charming parents at another company function.”

“I wouldn’t know.” She deftly deflected his question. “How do you like working with my sister?”

“She’s a promising young lawyer. I appreciate her stands on environmental issues, even if I don’t always agree with them.”

“I live in Dillon, so I worry about oil exploration in the mountains. You know, like fracking.”

He scowled. “I don’t know why people get up in arms about fracking. The process is effective and efficient.”

“Except for destroying the environment and polluting the water table,” she shot back. “Not to mention the possibility of earthquakes.”

Clark launched into a lecture that rang true for a somewhat condescending executive of an energy company. His speech was more than a performance. After his years undercover, he had taken on the characteristics of his profession. Troy had to wonder how long it had been since Clark, alias Kruger, had been involved in espionage that involved anything more complicated than the transfer of funds.

“I didn’t mean to offend you,” Olivia said

sweetly. "My sister wouldn't represent CRG Energy unless you were a responsible company. You're one of the good guys."

"Of course," he said. "Tell me your parents' opinion. Have they ever mentioned me? Or CRG?"

"Not that I recall."

"I think you know a great deal more than you're willing to admit."

Troy's nerves twitched. Clark's statement came close to a threat. He was tempted to take this guy into custody right now and damn the consequences.

"However," Clark continued, "I'm sure your condition consumes most of your attention."

"My condition?"

He cast a pointed gaze at the magnificent swell of her belly under her flowing gown. "My congratulations, by the way."

"I assure you that my pregnancy hasn't stopped my brain from functioning."

"Certainly not." He gave a nod. "Delighted to meet you. Have a lovely evening."

As he pivoted and walked into the crowd, Troy watched. If Clark left, he needed to send that text. "I think he's actually leaving."

"Good riddance," she muttered. "Let's find those crab cakes."

Her father appeared beside them. In a low

voice, he said, "Clark's heading out. I need to tail him. Give me your car keys."

No way would Troy send Olivia's father on this mission without a partner. He glanced around the room at the waiters who might be in disguise, unknown guests and the armed security entourage for the Saudi prince. Leaving Olivia alone here wasn't a good option; he could only be sure of her safety if he was at her side.

He tucked his hand under her arm. "Let's go. I'm driving."

"Wait!" She balked.

"I promise to get you more crab cakes."

"It's not that." She kicked off her high heels. "Would you grab those for me?"

Carrying her heels, he headed toward the door.

Chapter Twelve

Glad to be leaving the party, Troy hustled Olivia and her father across the manicured grounds to the service entrance where he'd parked the Range Rover. The delivery van with the fake-looking logo that he'd seen before was gone. Two men in chef outfits were having a smoke by the rose bushes. One of them was on a cell phone. Had he been posted as a lookout? Troy would have liked to question them, but there wasn't time.

Though Olivia moved faster without her fancy shoes, she wasn't exactly sprinting. She was gasping for breath as he opened the door to the backseat for her.

"I want to sit up front," she said.

"You're safer in back."

And her father had already vaulted into the front seat. "We need to hurry, dear."

She climbed inside, grumbling. "Didn't you say something about how you'd keep me informed?"

Leaning into the car for a quick kiss on her cheek, he whispered, "Trust me."

As he came around to the driver's side, he took out his phone and sent the text message to the forensic team at Clark's condo. They needed to evacuate. Troy hoped they'd found the evidence they needed.

Behind the steering wheel, he started the car. "All right, Richard. What's going on?"

"That's NTK."

"Need to know," Olivia translated from the backseat. "And it's a little late for that, Dad."

"This is so very wrong," Richard said. "I made a vow a long time ago to never put my children in danger. Yet, here you are, Olivia."

Troy pulled onto the street in time to see the taillights of a limo at the corner. "Is that Clark's car?"

"Yes," Richard said. "I saw him when we arrived. His driver was parked at the curb in front of the house and stood waiting by the vehicle."

"He was prepared for a fast getaway. Clark knows we're onto him."

"Possibly," Richard said.

"Who else knows?"

Olivia's father said nothing. Troy could appreciate his professionalism. It was Richard's job to hold tight to his secrets, never sharing intelligence with anyone but his wife. But this situation was different, and Troy was in no mood to play games.

"Right now," Troy said, "I'm your partner."

"And Olivia?"

"We keep her safe. That's our number one concern. Agreed?"

Richard exhaled a long-held breath. "Shortly after I informed my people that Clark was Kruger, the information leaked. His cover was blown. There were other people at this event who knew his identity."

Troy's gut instincts had been right on target. "Were they watching Clark? Or keeping an eye on us?"

"Both," Richard said. "My orders are to follow Clark and make sure that nothing happens to him until we take him into custody. Kruger, alias Clark, could be a valuable asset."

Fortunately, Troy's orders were much the same. "I was supposed to watch Clark and not interfere with him. We need the information he has about the Hatari terrorist cell and their potential target."

From the backseat, Olivia piped up. "I don't see his taillights. Did you lose him?"

"I'm being careful," Troy said. "I don't want to spook him. It looks like he's headed to his condo."

"Where is it?" she asked.

"He has a penthouse suite at a new building near Broadway." They weren't far from the location. He sped up and darted along a parallel street, catching sight of Clark's limo at an intersection.

"The penthouse sounds pretty posh," she said, "but I'm surprised Clark doesn't have a mansion. He's got to be a gazillionaire."

"The mansion is in Midland, Texas," her father said. "He also has a house in the Canadian oil fields. It's part of his cover. Being able to continually leave the U.S. for business abroad makes it easier for him to disguise his travel schedule."

"And he has a place in the mountains, as well," she said.

"How do you know that?" Troy ran a red light so he'd get the jump on Clark's driver.

"He mentioned it when he was trying to justify tearing up the landscape to suck out all the oil. Weren't you listening?"

"I was preparing to act as a referee. You and Clark were starting to get into it."

"His attitude ticks me off," she said. "So pretentious. He referred to his home in Aspen as a residence."

Too bad for Clark. The place he'd be living for the rest of his life would most likely be a prison cell—a room without a view.

Troy's driving maneuvers were successful. They arrived at the condo building before Clark's limo. The area was mostly residential with nice older homes and plenty of trees. The twenty-story condo was the only large structure, but there were a couple of three-story square brick apartment buildings. Both had lots, and Troy parked in a slot facing the street. From there, they had a clear view of the ramp that led down to a garage door for underground parking at the condo.

He killed the headlights and turned to Richard. "When are your guys going to make the arrest?"

"I made contact when I knew Clark was leaving the party. They should be ready to pick up this package." Olivia's father scanned up and down the street. "I don't see anybody, but that doesn't mean they aren't here."

"Call them."

If the CIA had the situation covered, Troy would be happy to stand down. He wasn't in a position to contact or give orders to the forensic team who had searched the condo. His only way of reaching them was via text message.

Richard disconnected his call. "They're only a few minutes away."

They should have been here, waiting. If Troy had been in charge, he would have made the arrest as soon as they had reason to confirm the identity. Letting a suspect run around loose was asking for trouble. "Why did they wait?"

Richard shrugged. "I don't know their tactics."

Troy was itching to make a move, but Olivia was with him. The right place for him to be was at her side. Still, it didn't hurt to be prepared. He flipped open the glove compartment and took out two automatic handguns, both Glocks.

"I want you both to stay in the car," he instructed. "If there's a threat, I need to be more mobile."

"Good plan," Richard said. "I'll come around to the driver's seat."

"I can drive," Olivia said.

The two men responded with one voice. "No."

In her tight-lipped expression, Troy saw the image of the little girl she'd once been—the child who wouldn't let her mother's kidnappers get away without her. All grown up, she was still stubborn, still determined, still strong. She was an outstanding woman. Soon, she'd be an outstanding mother.

"I'm proud of you," he said.

"Don't get hurt. Please, Troy, don't get hurt."

"That's not my plan. I'm just going to watch. When the CIA gets here, I'll back off and we'll go home. No problem."

He left the car and slid through the shadows. A holster was clipped to his belt. The other Glock was in his hand. He crouched, listening. A summer breeze ruffled tree branches, and an undercurrent of urban noise hummed around him. No one was on the street. If others were hiding out here, they were stealthier than ninjas.

Being outside and taking some kind of action felt good. His senses went on high alert. Adrenaline pumped through his blood. Troy never had the patience and subtlety to handle the kind of work Olivia's parents did. He liked having a direct mission with a clear directive. *Keep Clark safe. Keep him from falling into enemy hands.* Simple.

The limousine rounded the corner, heading toward the ramp for the underground garage. Troy figured that the driver would hit the remote control that opened the garage door, they'd drive inside, and all would be fine.

But the door didn't open. The driver stopped the vehicle in the middle of the street.

Troy was four car lengths away from the limo, too far to see inside and know what the driver was doing. But it was obvious that things weren't going as expected.

The smart move would be for the driver to hit the gas and zoom away fast. Under his breath, Troy whispered, "Go. Get the hell out of here."

In his undercover identity, Clark/Kruger hadn't been in action in a long time. He'd grown soft. A frightened man could make stupid mistakes.

Troy watched the limo drive toward the corner stop sign and signal a left turn. Big mistake. There could be an ambush at the front entrance to the condo building. After signaling Richard to stay put, he darted through the shadows and peered around the edge of the building at landscaping of thick shrubs and a tall spruce tree. He spotted an armed man dressed in black with a knit cap pulled low on his forehead and a half dozen tattoos on his exposed forearm. Well, damn. That outfit sure as hell wasn't standard CIA issue. Clark's enemies had caught up to him.

With his back against the wall of the building, Troy looked back toward the Range Rover. They had narrowly escaped disaster. If he'd parked at this end of the block, his vehicle would have drawn fire.

He turned toward the entrance where the limo was pulling to a stop. There was no way of knowing how many men were involved, but he was surely outnumbered and outgunned. If he opened fire, he'd be a dead man. His advantage was that they didn't know he was here. Moving fast, he approached the man in black. The guy didn't hear him, didn't turn around.

Using a maneuver he'd done a hundred times before, Troy took the guy out with a sleeper hold. The unconscious man slipped silently to the ground. Troy tossed aside his handguns and took possession of his AK-47, noting that it was a new version being manufactured in China. On the ground at his feet were four grenades. All this hardware for Clark? The ambush obviously wasn't meant to take him alive.

Troy peered through the branches of the spruce tree. Any minute now, the CIA would be here. *And they'll be too late.*

The driver got out of the limo and opened the rear door for Clark. Two shots echoed on the city street. The driver fell.

Clark managed to pull the door closed, but now he was stuck in the rear of the limo. Bullets pinged against the side of the vehicle. The safety glass in the windows wouldn't last much longer. Clark was pinned down. No way could he escape.

Observing the flash from the AK-47 weapons, Troy guessed that there were two other assailants. Both were on the opposite side of the building's entrance.

The gunfire ceased. A grenade was lobbed through the air. Floating like an underhand softball pitch, it bounced off the hood of the limo. The explosion tore away the grill and front bumper on the passenger side.

This firefight wasn't going to last more than a few minutes so Troy had no reason to hold back. He threw all four of the grenades in the direction of the gunfire. Fireballs exploded. Over the roar of the concussion, he heard a man scream.

Gunfire and grenades were going to be aimed in his direction. He let go with a blast from the

AK-47 and dodged behind the brick wall of the building. While he was trying to decide whether to step into the line of fire and engage, he heard sirens. Reinforcements were there. None too soon.

The CIA arrived first. Half a dozen guys in bulletproof vests took over the fight. There was more to this fight, but Troy had done his bit. He needed to make sure nobody else ran in the direction of the Range Rover. He needed to be sure Olivia was safe.

As he dashed across the street to where he had parked, she emerged from the vehicle and ran barefoot in his direction. What the hell was she doing? Hadn't she heard the explosions? Was she deliberately ignoring danger?

He swept her into his arms. "Get back in the car."

"Are you all right?" Her eyes were wild. "Tell me you're all right."

"Not until you're in the car." He shoved her into the backseat and dived in behind her, slamming the door behind him.

She held his face in both her hands. "You scared me half to death."

"I'll need to get this suit dry-cleaned for my brother. Other than that, I'm fine."

Her mouth pressed gently against his. His pulse was still racing. He was breathing hard. The extreme pressure of battle clenched inside him, tying his gut into knots. But the sweetness of her kiss did a lot to ease his tension. Every fight should end with a kiss from a beautiful woman as a reminder of what was really important.

In the front seat, Richard cleared his throat. "Do you mind telling me what happened?"

"Your guys finally got here." Troy continued to focus on Olivia. He tucked a strand of long blond hair behind her ear. "I've never been so glad to see a swarm of agents in bulletproof vests with CIA stenciled across the back."

"What about Clark? Is he still alive?"

"I don't know."

Troy slumped back against the seat and pulled Olivia across his lap. He wanted to take her home and spend the rest of the night in her arms, but that wasn't going to be possible. He had witnessed the ambush; the CIA would have a lot of questions for him.

And Troy had his own agenda. He took out his cell phone and texted a message. Ambush at Clark's condo. Need backup. If Clark was still alive, they needed all the intelligence they could get on the Hatari terrorist cell.

Chapter Thirteen

A pregnant woman in a lavender ball gown wasn't something anyone expected to find at a crime scene. Olivia knew she was drawing stares from the CIA agents, the cops, the ambulance EMTs, the firemen and the mysterious investigators who spoke only to Troy. They'd all be a lot happier if she hitched up her skirts and left. But that wasn't going to happen.

She needed to talk to Matthew Clark, and she refused to go away until she looked him straight in the eye and asked him if he was behind the kidnap attempt that had thrown her life into chaos. *One lousy question.* That was all she wanted.

In her bare feet, she stood across the street from the twenty-story condo building. Her toes dug into the cool grass. Everything was drenched when the fire trucks extinguished the flames from the explosions. Water ran down the gutters and glistened on the pavement. Police lights illuminated the crime scene. There were watchers standing on the other side of the yellow tape.

Several of the vehicles parked along the street had been burned and mangled. Clark's limo was the worst. The gas tank had caught fire and exploded, leaving a twisted hunk of metal that looked like a mad sculptor's vision of a post-apocalyptic world. And yet, Matthew Clark had escaped without a scratch. Life really wasn't fair.

His driver and one other man were dead. An ambulance with siren screaming had driven off with two other injured men. One of the fire trucks had also left. A second truck and the crew stayed behind to deal with the fire damage that had scorched the bricks on the first floor of the condo building and had broken several windows.

Troy separated from the mob of investigators and came toward her. Though he was a mess with soot smeared across his clothes and face, he bristled with vitality. The man was in his element; he felt at home in a war zone.

He slipped his arm around her shoulder. "I'd really like to take you home."

"Not until I see Clark."

"I don't know what you expect to get from him. He's lived a lie for most of his life. What makes you think he'll tell you the truth?"

"I'll know." She looked toward the panel van where the CIA had sequestered Clark. "I don't know why, but I feel like I'll know if he's lying or telling the truth."

He gave her shoulder a squeeze. "Your dad is doing everything he can to get you five minutes with Clark. He's calling in favors from high-level people."

"The way I figure," she said, "the CIA owes me."

"How so?"

"Simple logic." It made perfect sense to her. "Because Clark came after me, you and my parents were working together. You pulled up a photo, and Mom recognized him. If I hadn't been involved, you never would have met. They owe me."

"Yeah, I get it," he said. "Keep in mind that the CIA can be damn unreasonable. If they turn Clark to their side, he'll be a valuable asset."

"I'm not going to break him."

"I doubt you could. He seems to be indestructible." Troy's gaze rested on the grotesque remains of the limo. "From what I heard, Clark exited the vehicle just before it blew."

But his driver was killed. Again, she thought, life wasn't fair. "Do they know who arranged the ambush?"

"If they do, they're not telling. The significant fact is that there's a traitor. Somebody passed on the intelligence about Kruger being Clark real fast." He looked toward the van where Clark was being held. "The only reason the CIA hasn't zoomed away with their precious asset is because the forensic team I was working with won't let them. They want Clark."

"And who are they?"

"I'm not sure. There are so many supposedly elite departments and supposedly elite intelligence units that you can't tell who's who. I mean, look at this mess. It's a circus."

She had to agree. There were police officers in uniform, CIA agents in windbreakers, crime scene investigators with flashlights, plainclothes detectives and other people with badges she couldn't identify. "You don't like the circus?"

"Not unless I'm going to see a pretty lady in tights on the flying trapeze." He gestured toward a nearby bench at the bus stop. "Let's sit down."

"I'd rather stand." She didn't want to fade into the background. Though nobody was paying much attention to her anymore, they were aware of her presence. "How does Clark's capture affect your terrorist cell?"

"Here's the best-case scenario. Clark tells us the location where they're planning to strike. We move in. Take Hatari into custody. The threat is over."

"And the worst case?"

He shook his head. "They carry out their plot."

"Have you talked to Sergeant Nelson?"

"Nelson and the rest of my team are in New York. Because of our connection to Hatari, we're right in the middle and ready to take action."

She heard a note of disappointment in his voice. "Do you want to be with them?"

"They're my men. I want to support them, but I need to be here." His smile seemed a little forced. "I'm not leaving you."

She rested her head against his shoulder. "If I could talk to Clark, I'd know if he was behind the kidnap attempt. I'd know whether I was still in danger."

"And?"

"If nobody is trying to grab me, there's no reason for you to stay here and protect me."

"You're wrong about that." He reached down and patted her belly. "This is my reason."

Her dad came toward them. Though everybody else was grimy, he still looked neat and spiffy in his party duds. She could tell by his expression that he didn't have good news.

"The CIA is taking Clark," he said. "They can't let you talk to him now, but they might arrange a meeting tomorrow."

She watched the van holding Clark drive away. "Is he talking? Has he admitted to being Kruger?"

"He's said nothing."

"But he's under arrest, right?"

"Technically, he's being held in connection with a possible terrorist action."

She wasn't sure what that meant. "What's the difference?"

"In this circumstance, Miranda rights don't apply. He doesn't have access to a lawyer."

"That's probably a good thing." Her sister's firm represented CRG Energy and could be called to handle this case. "I'm pretty sure Bianca wouldn't want to defend this guy."

"She wouldn't have to. Matthew Clark is a wealthy man. He can afford a dream team of lawyers if that's the way he chooses to play the situation."

Her father deflated as he exhaled a sigh. It had been a long, frustrating day for her, and she imagined it was even worse for him. After revealing his CIA identity to his daughters, his life would never be the same. He would no longer have a veil of secrecy to hide behind.

She took her father's arm. "Let's go home."

BACK AT HER sister's house, Olivia tried to cuddle with Troy on the twin beds they'd pushed together. It wasn't going well. No matter how they arranged themselves, one or the other of them slipped into the crack between the beds.

"If I wasn't pregnant," she muttered, "this would work. Maybe we can sleep crosswise."

"And have our butts stuck between the beds?"

She knew that Bianca was sleeping on a lovely king-size bed in her own bedroom, but she couldn't ask her sister to give up her comfortable space. "Poor Bianca. She's a wreck."

"Understandable." As he tried to get closer the beds pushed farther apart. "Her law firm can't be happy about what happened to Matthew Clark."

Making Bianca's situation even worse was the need for secrecy. If she told her bosses that her parents were CIA field agents, their cover was blown—a serious situation that would put all their international contacts in jeopardy. Bianca had to stick with a lie to explain why her dad, Olivia and Troy had been at the crime scene where Clark was taken into custody. They'd said they were following Matthew Clark to his condo for a drink, and then they'd gotten swept up in the ambush and were questioned by the police as witnesses.

Olivia figured it was the first of many lies that her sister would have to tell. "Mom and Dad were right. It was easier when we didn't know they were CIA."

"Both you and your sister had a pretty good idea of what they did."

"Suspecting is different from knowing."

"If it's any consolation," he said, "I think your

dad is ready for retirement. If Clark/Kruger turns out to be a valuable asset, his capture makes a good swan song for Richard and Sharon Laughton."

"I hope so." She gave up trying to get close and pushed against his chest. "You go over there on the other side of the crack. I want to talk."

As he repositioned himself, he turned on the bedside lamp and checked his cell phone for messages. Ever since he'd heard that his men were in New York, Troy had been distracted. He'd taken two more calls from Sergeant Nelson, giving him updates on the tracking of the Hatari terrorists.

When he turned toward her, the pastel flowered sheet slipped lower on his hips. The ridiculous, girlie bed linens emphasized his masculinity. He was shirtless, and the glow from the lamp burnished his muscular shoulders. On his side, he cocked his arm and rested his cheek on his fist.

"Don't worry about your sister," he said. "She'll be okay."

"How do you know?"

"She's tough like you, and she's a lawyer, accustomed to thinking before she speaks."

"That's not like me," she said. "I tend to blurt."

"You act from your heart, from instinct."

His analysis was on target. She didn't spend much time thinking and worrying. She just knew. "I wish there was something I could do about Bianca and the prince. It's obvious that they're attracted to each other."

"You might want to stay out of it."

"Or I might want to buy her a plane ticket to his country and have her delivered to him wearing a big red bow and nothing else." She grinned at him and wiggled her eyebrows. "It worked pretty well for me when I turned up on your doorstep and jumped you."

"I want to thank you for that."

He wasn't laughing, didn't even smile. His eyes reflected a steady, cool glow that was a little bit disconcerting. "Troy? What are you thinking? Don't get all serious."

"Making love to you that night might be the best thing that ever happened to me," he said. "I'm glad it worked out pretty well for you, too."

A wave of warmth washed over her. She felt herself melting. In the past couple of days, they'd gotten to know each other so much better. She never would have pegged him as an understanding man. But he was. Tough and protective when he needed to be. But Troy was also kind.

As she reached toward him, the diamond in her ring flashed. Their engagement charade was over and she ought to give the ring back, but maybe she'd keep it. Just for tonight.

He caught her hand, brought her fingers to his

lips and brushed a light kiss across her knuckles. His gaze was mesmerizing.

She stretched toward him, and he did the same. In the gap between the beds, their lips met for a light, tantalizing kiss that sent shivers through her. Her hand slipped from his grasp. She touched his shoulder, his forearm. When she traced her fingernails across the hard muscles of his chest, he gasped.

The distance between them was less than two feet, but it felt like she was reaching for miles. Each physical contact seemed special and unique, almost magical.

He gently cupped her swollen breast. She closed her eyes, imagining a dream lover. His caresses were perfect. The sensations he aroused were erotic and comforting at the same time.

His cell phone buzzed.

His touch went cold. When she opened her eyes, she saw his tension.

"I have to take the call," he said.

"Of course."

While he picked up his cell phone, she rose from the bed, walked to the window and pushed aside the flowered drape so she could look out at the moonlit street. Her sister's house was air-conditioned so the window was closed, and Olivia wished she could open it. In the mountains, she always had her windows open. She missed the natural sounds of the night, missed her cabin, missed her daily routine.

Across the room, Troy paced in a tight circle. His voice was calm and controlled as he talked to Nelson on the phone, but his gestures were agitated. His fist clenched. His back tensed, and she watched the ripple of muscles across his shoulders. He looked good, wearing nothing but a pair of black boxers. If their relationship had been about nothing but sexual attraction, she wouldn't have hesitated to jump in with both feet.

But it was far more complicated. They were having a baby together, and she really wasn't sure if a man like Troy could be part of a family unit. His work was so important to him. Being a marine identified him. Earlier this evening when she watched him stroll through the crime scene, she'd seen a warrior, confident and strong.

She twisted the engagement ring on her finger. Could she live with a warrior? A man who constantly put his life on the line? Though he'd said he intended to retire from the field, she doubted that plan would stick. Settling down wasn't what men like Troy did. They needed action. She knew it was killing him to be here with her when his team was going into conflict.

Disconnecting his call, he strode toward her. "The chatter from Hatari went silent. They must have found out that Matthew Clark is in custody."

"What does that mean?"

"Could be a good thing." The worry lines across his forehead told her that he thought otherwise. "They might abort the mission. Or they could change the timing or the location where they intend to attack. We can only speculate."

"You should go to New York," she said. "You want to be with your men, and you should be."

He rested one hand on her shoulder. "Are you trying to get rid of me?"

"I won't stand in the way of your work." Never in her life had she played the role of a damsel in distress, and she wasn't about to start now. "You don't have to stay here to protect me. I promise to be careful."

"It's too dangerous. You saw the aftermath of what could happen. The burned, twisted metal. The dead and injured."

"They aren't after me." She threw up her hands in frustration. "I don't want to be here anymore. Being watched over makes me feel claustrophobic. I can't go for a walk if I feel like it. Can't even open a window in this house."

"It's a drag," he agreed.

"Don't get me wrong," she said. "I'm grateful to my sister for giving me a safe place to stay. And to my parents for being concerned. And to you..." She stared into his deep, dark eyes. "I'm especially grateful to you. This time with you has been good, really good."

"But it isn't what you want."

"All along I've planned to have the baby at my cabin. I've got everything arranged. A midwife friend of mine will come over and help." She had envisioned a peaceful atmosphere in the mountains, surrounded by her favorite things, listening to music she loved. "I just want to go home."

"That's what I want, too. I want to be with you for the birth of our son."

Though she hadn't included Troy in her original plans, things were different between them now. She liked the idea of having him with her. "When can we leave?"

"Soon." He slipped his arms around her. "Very soon."

Chapter Fourteen

By eleven o'clock the next morning, Olivia's frustration had built to an unbearable level. Though her sister's house had plenty of room, she felt like the walls were shrinking and she couldn't turn a corner without bumping into one of her family members. They were breaking down the wall of secrets, but they hadn't developed the knack of talking honestly to each other. Instead of admitting that they were scared or had needs, they smiled politely and looked away.

She found Troy in the living room where he'd made a comfortable nest at the end of the leather sofa. He was reading a sports magazine and drinking black coffee from a mug. She sat next to him. "Do you think my family is excessively nervous?"

"What do you mean?"

"Well, look at us. Bianca decided to work from home but can't stay in her home office because she doesn't want to miss anything. My dad keeps roaming from room to room while he talks on his cell phone and mutters to himself."

"He's got a lot on his plate," Troy said, defending her father. "Arranging access so we can talk to Clark, trying to identify the attackers from last night, and damage control to make sure the Laughton family cover story is safe."

"And my mom," she said. "She's puttering and actually doing housework. Believe me, that's not her thing."

"What about you?" he asked.

"Well, let's see." She tapped the side of her head with her forefinger. "I've eaten breakfast, watched TV, read a bit, and gone back to the kitchen to forage. I'm as jumpy as the rest of them. Do you think we're all as crazy as bedbugs?"

"A lot of secrets got spilled, and that's hard to deal with." He gave her a grin. "I have a suggestion."

"I thought you might." In contrast to her family, Troy was calm and self-possessed. The only hint of tension was his obsession with answering his cell phone, which never left his sight. "Tell me."

"Since I pretty much destroyed the suit I borrowed from my brother, I wanted to visit Alex and find out the name of his dry cleaner. Do you want to come with me to the clinic?"

"Can we leave right now?"

When he took his car keys from his pocket and jingled them, she responded with the enthusiasm of a dieter hearing a dinner bell. After quickly telling her mom where they were going, Olivia exited with Troy.

The cloudless day was hot but it felt good. She enjoyed the warmth of the sun on her arms and bare legs. A clear, golden light spread across the lawns and drew the heads of dahlias and asters upward. As soon as she was belted into the passenger seat of the Range Rover, she lowered the window, preferring the fresh air to the cool of air-conditioning.

"I feel so free," she said. "That's kind of an exaggeration, isn't it? Spending one morning with my family isn't exactly like being in prison."

"You can always blame it on the hormones," he said drily.

"So true."

Their trip to the clinic wasn't going to be all fun and games. Carol Rainer was the clinic's new receptionist, and Olivia wasn't sure what would happen when they met again. The last time she'd seen Carol was in the hospital while she was recovering from the accident. They'd only spoken for a few moments. Carol had been too drugged up to make sense, and Olivia had been so devastated that all she could do was apologize again and again.

Almost nine months had passed, and Olivia had changed. She rested her hand on her belly. Her life was different now. And Carol? The fact that she was working at a clinic for the homeless meant that she'd made changes, too.

The clinic was located in a converted warehouse that was less than a mile away from the fashionable LoDo area of Denver. Though the windows on the dark brick building were washed and the sidewalk swept, there was nothing chic about this small health care facility. This wasn't an emergency room, and they had no drugs on the premises. In this dodgy neighborhood, having anything stronger than aspirin was an invitation to robbery.

The purpose of the clinic was to diagnose, handle small problems, give free flu shots and refer patients to low-cost options for treatment. When Olivia was coming to Denver on a regular, twice-a-month basis, she offered prenatal and postnatal classes for moms in addition to giving exams. Once, she had delivered a baby here, but that had been an emergency.

Troy parked the Range Rover in a slanted space in front of a plumbing supply warehouse down the block from the clinic. Before opening his door, he checked the mirrors and looked over his shoulder. "We weren't followed."

She'd almost forgotten the danger. "Are you sure?"

"If we'd picked up a tail, I'd know." He reached across the console and took her hand. "Are you okay with seeing Carol again?"

Her big, tough marine hated when she cried. "There might be tears."

"Copy that."

"I don't know what else to expect."

The trauma and tragedy of the accident had been so intense that she might never find closure. To tell the absolute truth, she didn't really want to face Carol Rainer, but she couldn't turn her back and walk away when Carol had made an effort to contact her. As she left the Range Rover and went into the clinic, Olivia braced herself.

The receptionist desk in the front waiting room was empty, but Carol squatted on the floor, refereeing a game between two toddlers in saggy diapers. She looked up when the door opened. When she saw Olivia, she stared for a few seconds until recognition set in.

Like a shot, Carol bounced to her feet and flew across the dingy tile floor. She wrapped Olivia in a tight hug and whispered, "I've thought about you so many times."

"Me, too."

Tears spilled down her cheeks. Holding Carol brought back images. Olivia remembered the blood, the horror and the desperation as she fought to save the lifeless infant. But there were other times, better times. She remembered Carol laughing with her auburn hair pulled up in a ponytail and her pregnant belly bulging. There had been a day in Carol's spacious kitchen when they talked about prenatal vitamins and baked cinnamon snickerdoodles.

Reluctantly, Olivia ended the hug and swabbed the tears from her cheeks. Carol did the same.

"You've got to tell me," Olivia said. "How did you end up working here?"

"Because of you."

"Me?"

In spite of her smile, Carol's green eyes held a dark edge of pain that Olivia had seen in other parents who had lost children. "I wanted to get together with you, but there's no chance that I'm ever going back to Dillon. I remembered you talking about the clinic in Denver, and I came here."

"That explains how you got there, but why did you stay?"

"When I walked in the door, the place was total chaos. There were a dozen people waiting to be seen, and the receptionist had to leave. I offered to help out, and she gladly handed over the reins. Very gladly, I must say. She couldn't wait to get out of here. But I liked the idea of doing something useful. And I was totally convinced when

Alex came racing out of the back examination area, gave me one of his killer smiles and asked if I wanted a job."

"That's my bro." Troy shook her hand. "I'm Troy Weathers."

"I should have known. You look a lot alike." Carol's gaze focused on Olivia's left hand. "Is he your fiancé?"

Explaining seemed too complicated. Olivia forced a smile. "You could say that."

"Congratulations. You're getting married. Having a baby. I'm happy for you."

Olivia wished she could say the same. Carol had lost her baby, and it sounded like her marriage was no longer intact. Though Olivia could have dismissed the memories of the accident and pretended that she and Carol were nothing more than old friends, she didn't want to bury those feelings. Taking Carol's hand, she led her behind the reception desk, leaving Troy to entertain the two toddlers.

"After the accident," Olivia said, "tell me what happened."

"I was in bad shape, physically and emotionally. There were moments when I just wanted to die. As soon as I could get around in a wheelchair, we had a funeral. My son's name was Arthur James Rainer. I buried him in a tiny white coffin."

As she spoke, her shoulders slumped but her eyes were dry. This woman had been through the worst nightmare a parent could endure but it hadn't destroyed her. She continued, "I'll always love Arthur James. I don't understand why he's gone, but he is. It was an accident. I don't blame Jarvis or myself, and I certainly don't blame you, Olivia. That was why I wanted to see you. I needed to tell you that it wasn't your fault."

"I share your grief, Carol."

"I know you do." She gazed at Olivia's belly. "I hope we can share in good times, too. I want you to consider me your friend."

"What's happened between you and your husband?"

"The last time I saw him was at the funeral. Our marriage was rocky before I got pregnant. The accident ended any affection we had for each other. Jarvis actually threatened to sue me for not wearing my seat belt in the accident."

"I'm so sorry." What a horrible thing to do to a grieving mother!

"Don't be. For me, that threat was the last straw. My lawyer is going to take Jarvis for a boatload of money, maybe even part of his oil business." She grinned. "I might be making a nice, juicy donation to the clinic."

"Good for you."

Across the room, Olivia saw Troy answer his

cell phone. He signaled to her. "We need to go. That person we wanted to see last night has some time for us."

Matthew Clark. She took Carol's hand. "I'll be back later. If I don't see you then, I'll call. I want to stay in touch."

Olivia wasn't making an empty promise. There was an important lesson in her contact with Carol, something she needed to learn and to remember.

TROY KNEW HOW difficult it had been for Olivia's father to get this chance for them to interview Kruger, alias Matthew Clark. Security in the lockdown facility was intense with bomb-proof walls, no windows and armed guards. Several different law enforcement agencies were doing their damnedest to make sure nobody got a second chance to kill this man.

As Troy watched Olivia with her blond hair tumbling carelessly around her shoulders and her khaki shorts and her cute blue blouse with ruffles, he was struck by how out of place she was in this grim, gray environment. She ought to be posing for a portrait of serenity. Not facing a renowned international spy.

Two guards escorted them into the room where Kruger/Clark was being held. The only furniture in the cell was a table and several hardback chairs, but it didn't look like Kruger was being treated badly. He wasn't shackled, and he wore his own clothing.

He rose from behind the table, nodded a greeting and offered a friendly smile. "I've been told that this lovely lady is responsible for my capture."

"That's correct," she said. Her tone was ice-cold. Her eyes were determined and hard. Troy recognized the velvet-and-steel resemblance to her mom.

"But you're not the spy in the family, are you?" Kruger/Clark sat behind the table and crossed his legs. "I should have known from the first time I met your parents and your sister introduced them as diplomats that they were spies."

Troy said, "You should have known a lot of things, Kruger."

"Please call me Clark," he said. "I've grown accustomed to the name and the lifestyle. I'm going to miss my home in Aspen. Olivia, dear, you live in the mountains. You know how lovely it is in the autumn."

"We're not here to give you information," Troy said.

"I know exactly what you want, Captain Weathers. You're worried about my friends in Hatari, and you should be. They're scary, even to me. And, sorry to say, I don't know their target."

Troy knew he'd already been questioned about

the terrorist cell and had claimed ignorance of their motives or moves. "That's the line you're sticking with?"

"It's the truth."

Clark was a professional liar, clever enough to have hidden his identity for over twenty years. Troy would have welcomed the opportunity to question Clark in depth. But they had only five minutes, and Olivia had first dibs on their time. He pulled a chair away from the table and indicated that she should sit. "Ask your questions."

She sat straight in the chair with her shoulders back. Her hands rested on her thighs. "You claimed that you didn't know my parents worked for the CIA. Is that a lie?"

"I must say, it's refreshing to talk to you. No subtlety. None at all."

"Did you know my parents were spies?"

"No."

His sly smile was ambiguous. At the party when they'd talked to him, Clark had been scared. Now, he acted with the arrogance of someone who thought he was the smartest guy in the room.

"Obviously," she said, "you know Captain Weathers. Were you aware of his relationship to me?"

"Why on earth would I care?" His mouth curved in a sneer. "The marines were concerned with Hatari. They knew nothing about me."

Not true. Though Troy and his team didn't know that Kruger was Clark, they'd picked up a line on Kruger being the financier for Hatari through computer chatter. Was Clark testing him? Trying to get a rise from him?

A good interrogator could get a suspect to open up. A great one was better than a shot of truth serum. Troy wasn't great, but he had some experience, and he only needed one answer from Clark: Where will Hatari strike?

Olivia asked, "How did you know that I live in the mountains?"

"You mentioned it when we were chatting at the party."

"Oh, I guess I did."

Troy could see that she was beginning to be flustered, and he took advantage. His best tactic with Clark was to make him think they were no threat.

Sitting in the chair beside Olivia, he took his eyes off Clark and focused on her. "It's okay," he assured her. "You're doing fine."

"Adorable," Clark said with a smug grin. "You're a cute couple. When's the baby due?"

Anger tightened Olivia's jaw. She hated being patronized. "Your men were watching me," she said. "They followed us into Denver."

"Is that what this interview is about?"

Olivia demanded, "Did you plan to abduct me?"

"My dear girl, certainly not."

Clark's tone was relaxed. He thought he had this interview in the bag. Therefore, his guard was down. This was the time for Troy to make his move.

His team had consulted with other branches of intelligence. Together, they'd homed in on three possible locations for the terrorist strike. But there was another site—one that Troy had favored based on the Clark connection. This building in Manhattan was the corporate headquarters for one of CRG Energy's main competitors.

He looked into Clark's eyes. "Hazelwood Oil, Ritter Plaza, New York."

"Come again?"

He feigned indifference, but Troy had noticed the twitch of a muscle in the corner of his eye and a minuscule tremble of his lips. The location meant something to him.

The door behind them opened, and a guard announced, "Your time is up."

Troy stood. "I have what I need."

He deliberately turned his back on Clark, a show that the former spy was no longer worthy of his attention. As soon as he left this cell, he'd put in a call to Nelson and tell him that they needed to expand the parameters of their search.

He and Olivia were almost out the door when Clark spoke again. "One more thing."

They both turned to face him.

Clark's expression was a mask of disgust. "Olivia, dear, I had no intention of hurting you. But I might know someone who does."

"Give me a name," she demanded.

"You'll have to find out for yourself."

Troy suspected that Clark's statement was nothing more than a desperate attempt to gain the upper hand. But he couldn't ignore the threat.

Chapter Fifteen

After he made his call to Gunny Sergeant Nelson, Troy's plan was to take Olivia back to her sister's house where they would spend the rest of the day being safe and secure. With a little persuasion, he might convince her that the bedroom was the safest room in the house, and they could rest in each other's arms while he figured out what to do next.

She had a different idea.

"Food," she said as the Range Rover turned onto Colfax Avenue. "I'm starving."

"Your sister has food."

"Bianca has organic food," she muttered. "What I want is a hot dog and fries. Really greasy fries."

But she was a health nut. The night they'd ordered from room service she'd wanted fish and rice. "Greasy fries? That doesn't sound like you."

"Maybe it's not. Maybe this is a direct request from the uterus. The kid wants a dog. And, lucky us, we're driving along a street with lots of yummy choices."

She sounded too cheerful for someone who'd had her life threatened, and he wasn't sure what to make of her attitude. With her current tendency toward mood swings, he couldn't tell if she was trying to cover up her fear or really wasn't scared or was just plain hungry.

He needed to protect her. "When we talked to Clark, did—"

"He was telling the truth," she said with exasperation. "Good grief, Troy, this must be the twentieth time I've told you. Clark isn't after me, and he never was. I believe him."

"And why would you trust that snake?"

"Call it a gut feeling." She patted her belly. "And I've got quite a gut."

Optimism was one thing, but the way she was behaving was almost manically upbeat. "He also claimed to know someone who wanted to hurt you. Is that the truth?"

"When Clark said that, he was blowing smoke. You rattled him when you mentioned that oil company in New York, and he was trying to get back at you." She pointed at a hot dog stand. "Deli Dogs. That's what I want for lunch."

He'd rather take her to her sister's house with the state-of-the-art security system. "We're not that far from Bianca's."

"Pull over," she growled.

He drove into the parking lot, fearful that if he didn't feed her, she'd rip the steering wheel from his hands or start gnawing on the upholstery. Hopefully, she'd be more cooperative after she'd been fed.

Deli Dogs was a squat little diner, painted red-and-white. The concrete patio in the front had picnic tables with red umbrellas, but they wouldn't be sitting there. An open dining area made it too easy for a drive-by assault.

At the window inside, they ordered two Polish dogs each and cheese fries. "And pickles," she said. "Is that too big a pregnancy cliché? Wanting pickles?"

"Not unless you put them with ice cream."

She thought for a moment, and then shook her head. "Not this time."

They sat at one of the small tables, waiting for their order. Troy maintained vigilance, watching the people who came through the door and assessing their threat potential, but he was more concerned about Olivia. Her high energy level worried him. She was like a kite soaring into the atmosphere, and it was up to him to rein her in before she crashed into the treetops.

He took her hand. His thumb brushed across the diamond she was still wearing. "We need to talk about our meeting with Clark."

"Again?"

"It's important." He gazed steadily into her eyes. "We don't have a lot of clues to go on."

She had a talent for putting up a brave front, but he sensed her tension. Her pupils darted nervously, and her grin faltered. "Go ahead," she said. "Talk."

Rather than arguing, he decided to accept her so-called gut feeling. "Let's assume that Clark wasn't the person who ordered for you to be watched, pursued or abducted."

She nodded. "Okay."

"We know there's someone after you. We saw evidence at the cabin. And we were chased."

"Right again."

"Our problem is to figure out who the hell is after you. I see two possibilities. Either Clark knows of a conspiracy among other spies or there's some other kind of connection between you and him."

"A connection?"

"He knows somebody who wants to hurt you. Can you think of people you might know in common?"

"There's my sister, of course."

"Has Bianca introduced you to anybody else from her firm? Or from CRG Energy?"

"I've met a couple of people my sister works

with. Once, she tried to fix me up with a blind date, but our schedules were never in sync."

"So, nobody from the firm or from CRG," he concluded. "Think of other people you know. Can we rule out ex-boyfriends?"

"We've been over this before," she said. "I can't think of anybody who wants to hurt me. Of course I have ex-boyfriends. What woman doesn't? But none of them are psycho enough to try to abduct me. And none of them would have the financial means to set up a two-car chase."

She couldn't be sure of that. A two-car chase involving rental cars wasn't that costly. "Any bad breakups?"

"There was a guy I lived with for three months, a ski instructor. He was angry when I kicked him out, but it was mostly because he didn't want to look for another place to live rent-free. He wasn't obsessed with me or anything."

"A ski instructor might have come into contact with Clark. They might have met at his place in Aspen."

"I never thought of that," she said, "but it makes sense. It's like that six degrees of separation thing. I might know somebody who knows somebody who knows Clark."

Tracking that sort of tenuous connection was nearly impossible, but they had to try. "When we get back to your sister's house, you can make a list of everybody you know. We'll cross-reference with what we know of Clark."

Their order came up, and he carried the heavy-laden tray to their table. Though Deli Dogs posted notes on their menu claiming to be nitrate-free and pure beef, this plate was a junk food bonanza, which didn't seem to bother Olivia at all. She took giant bites. As she chewed, she made the kind of orgasmic groans he'd heard from her in bed. Her eyes rolled in sheer happiness.

Her guard was down, and he liked seeing her this way. When she didn't have an agenda, she was vulnerable and quirky—fun to be around. The more time they spent together, the more he wanted to be with her.

"I love..." He stopped himself before he said the wrong thing and sent her running in the opposite direction. "I love watching you eat."

She gave him a thumbs-up and pounced on her greasy fries.

AT HER SISTER'S house, Olivia felt safe—trapped but safe. Sitting around the table with her dad and Troy, she tried her best to follow the plan: listing everyone she knew who might also know Clark. The tally was surprisingly high. In her work, she came into contact with a number of doctors and hospital personnel who hobnobbed with the wealthy. Her clients came from all walks of life.

Her friends were other people who engaged in outdoor sports or other midwives.

"Nobody stands out," she said. "And none of these people have a motive to hurt me."

"You're doing very well," her dad said. "If I had a more comprehensive list of Clark's acquaintances, we might start seeing a pattern."

Troy's cell phone rang, and he excused himself to take the call from Sergeant Nelson. As he left the room, she turned to her father and asked, "Is this the kind of thing that spies do? Making lists and checking them twice?"

"Your mother and I usually pass our intelligence back to the analysts who use computers to make these connections. But ninety percent of our work isn't the least bit exciting."

"And the other ten percent?"

"The attack last night was more violence than I've seen in years," he admitted. "I hated it. The senseless destruction reminded me of how very out of practice I am when it comes to fieldwork. I can't tell you the last time I've taken target practice."

His eyes were red-rimmed and tired. Though he was still a healthy man, her dad was in his sixties, no longer in the prime of his life when it came to fighting the kind of battles that Troy faced. "It could be time for you to retire."

"CIA agents never really retire. The agency becomes part of our identity. But your mother and I will very likely become inactive, no longer taking on new assignments."

"And what does that mean?"

"Maybe we'll live in Paris. Your mother always liked France."

"I like art," her mom said as she came into the room. "But France will be too far away from my new grandson. I'm thinking of Santa Fe, New Mexico. Or Carmel in California."

"Or Aspen," her dad suggested.

"Or Baja."

"Or all of the above." Olivia didn't see her globe-trotting parents settling in one place for an extended period of time. "You'll definitely be cool grandparents."

Her mother gave her a hug and a kiss on the cheek. "I hate to think of you being in any sort of danger, but I'm so glad we've had this time together. Your father and I are delighted we can participate in the birthing process."

"Not so fast," Olivia said. "I'm not going to a hospital."

"Whatever you say, dear. I'm sure your sister and I can handle the arrangements. We'll do it right here."

As if giving birth was a dinner party? That wasn't what she wanted. Her time in labor shouldn't be arranged for everyone's convenience, and it shouldn't be an instructional guide for her mother and sister. Olivia wanted it her way. At her home. With a midwife she knew and trusted.

Troy stepped into the room and signaled to her. "Can we talk for a minute?"

She hoisted herself from the table and went toward him. Taking her hand, he led her all the way upstairs to their bedroom where they would have privacy. He must have something serious to discuss.

When he closed the door behind her, she was curious but still focused on what her mother had said. "When I give birth, it's not going to be here on twin beds that keep sliding apart. And I'm not going to a hospital."

"Whatever you say." He crossed to the window and looked down at the yard.

"I want to be at my cabin. I know it takes a village to raise a child, and I want everyone to share in this baby's life. But the birth is mine. It needs to be natural. I need to be at peace. You'll back me up on this, won't you?"

"If I can."

"What does that mean?" She studied his profile as he stared through the window at the afternoon sun. He seemed distracted. "Troy, what's wrong?"

"I just got off the phone with Nelson. My team has become an integral part of the search for the terrorist cell."

"Isn't that what you expected?" she asked. "Your men speak Swahili. They have firsthand knowledge of Hatari in Rwanda. It makes sense that they'd take the lead."

He pivoted and came toward her. The faint lines at the corners of his eyes deepened as he squinted. His mouth was a hard, stubborn line. "I want to be with them."

And not with me. For the past couple of days she'd been chafing under the restrictions of being protected, but she didn't want him to leave. "Tell me more."

"Do you remember when we were talking about my work and I told you my proudest accomplishment?"

"That you'd never lost a man."

"I trust my guys to do the right thing. They're savvy, and they're quick. But I need to be sure they're following the best leader. I can't let them risk their lives unless I'm there."

His words embodied her worst fears about having a relationship with him. His job put him in danger. She couldn't say goodbye with the knowledge that it might be for the last time. Damn it, she hadn't wanted to care about him. She'd known that it would only bring hurt.

He continued, "According to current information, the terrorist cell is going to attack tomorrow. I want to be there with my men."

"What about protecting me? You're the one who keeps telling me that I'm in danger."

"And you keep saying you aren't. That there's nobody who wants to hurt you. You believed Clark."

"Just because I don't wave my fear like a banner, it doesn't mean I'm not scared."

She turned away from him, hiding the tears that sprang to her eyes. Before she was pregnant, she never cried. Now, her eyes were a leaky faucet. Angrily, she dashed the moisture away. It was hard to admit that she wasn't in control of her life. She hated asking for help.

"You're right." He rested his hands on her shoulders and lightly massaged. "I won't leave. You're my first priority. I need to be here with you."

"Forget it." She shrugged off his hands. "I can take care of myself. That's who I am. An independent woman."

"I'm staying."

She whirled to face him. "Go. Get out of here. Do your damn job. That's what you want, what you live for."

"Nothing is more important to me than you and our son."

"I won't stand in your way or have you blaming me if—God forbid—something goes wrong in New York. You don't have any obligation to me. I can handle this."

He took a step back. "You've been pushing me away ever since you told me you were pregnant."

"I don't need you. I don't need anyone."

She saw the hurt in his eyes. An echo of his pain wrenched inside her, but she couldn't stop herself. The engagement ring tightened on her finger. She yanked it off.

"This is yours." She held out the diamond toward him. "I accepted it under false pretenses. Go ahead, take it."

He turned and strode toward the door. Before opening it, he paused. "You're wrong about not needing anyone. Any day now, you're going to have a child. And you'll never be alone again."

He left her standing in the middle of the room with the diamond in her hand.

Chapter Sixteen

Olivia thought of herself as a calm, grounded person. A nurse. A midwife. Someone her patients could look to for guidance. *But not anymore.* Gone was the steady hand. Gone was the reassuring voice. Gone, gone, gone. She was out of control.

She'd been acting crazy with her weepy eyes and her demands for hot dogs and pickles, not to mention the unexpected waves of sensuality. Her hormones appeared to be in charge, and they weren't very smart. She didn't know if she wanted Troy to go or to stay or to take her with him.

Only one thing was clear in her mind. She didn't want him to leave with her angry words ringing in his ears. Of course, she was irritated when he chose being with his team instead of staying with her. Losing him as a bodyguard didn't really bother her. While she was staying in her sister's secure house with both armed parents keeping watch, she felt safe enough. The real reason she wanted Troy to be here was because she could go into labor at any given moment. If he was in New York, he might miss the birth of their son.

She stood at the bedroom window, looking down on the front yard. Below her, Troy sat outside on the stoop, waiting for his brother to pick him up. Though it would have been expedient to return the rental vehicle at the airport, he left the Range Rover for her to drive. As if she had someplace to go? As if her parents would let her out of their sight?

If Troy stayed here, he could convince them to let her return to her home in the mountains with him. They trusted him more than they trusted her. If only he would stay…

Uncurling her fingers, she looked at the engagement ring nestled on her palm. He'd been proposing to her from the moment she told him she was going to have his baby. In spite of her constant rejections, he'd been undaunted. Now, when she finally wanted him, he was walking away.

His brother's car pulled up to the curb.

"No," she said.

In her less-than-graceful gait, she rushed from the bedroom and thudded down the staircase. Unmindful of the alarms, she opened the front door and charged down the sidewalk, catching up to Troy before he got into the car.

"Wait." She threw her arms around his neck and kissed him hard on the lips. "Promise you'll be back."

"That was my intention."

"I know it seems like I'm fighting you every step of the way." As she looked into his dark and somewhat confused eyes, she realized how much she cared for him. The thought of never being held in his arms completely unnerved her. "I'm afraid."

"Of what?"

I don't want to lose you. But she couldn't tell him. To admit how much she cared meant she needed him, and she couldn't allow herself to go down that path.

He smoothed a wisp of hair off her forehead. "Keep your phone with you all the time, and I'll call you every step of the way. You won't even know that I'm gone."

From the driver's seat, Alex called out, "I've got to break this up. Troy needs to hurry if he's going to make his flight."

Her arms slipped off his shoulders. She held the engagement ring between them. "Take it. When you come back, ask me to marry you again."

"And what will you say?"

"I promise that it'll be the last time you make that proposal."

He pocketed the ring, then leaned down and talked to her belly. "Hey, kid, don't come out until I'm back."

With a wave, he got into the passenger seat, headed into battle. Unable to stop him from being a hero, she watched the car pull away.

Her dad joined her at the curb and wrapped a comforting arm around her back. "Troy's a good man. He won't take unnecessary risks."

It was the necessary risks that bothered her. He wasn't going to New York for a stroll in Central Park. He and his team were facing a desperate terrorist cell.

She rested her head on her father's shoulder. "You're right. He is a good man, a really good man."

"You should go inside." He kissed her cheek. "Put your feet up and relax."

"I want…" She exhaled a sigh. "I want a giant glass of straight whiskey."

Knocking herself unconscious until Troy got back would have been a lovely solution. But she couldn't indulge that whim.

"Would you settle for a cup of tea?" her dad asked.

"Don't have another choice, do I? Did I set off the alarm when I ran out the door?"

"I caught it in time," he said. "I was just getting ready to leave. I need to ask you for the keys for the Range Rover. You're blocking my car."

"They're in my purse." Along with the cell phone she had promised to keep with her at all times. "I'll get them."

Upstairs in the bedroom, she found her purse. Though she liked her oversize handbag for carrying lots of stuff, her purse wasn't the best for handy access, and she needed to be able to grab her cell phone at any given moment. She slipped her phone into the pocket of her khaki-colored cargo shorts with the pregnant waistband that stretched to infinity.

Keys in hand, she went downstairs to where her father waited. Before she handed them over, she asked, "Where are you going?"

"This is business."

Since his job was spying, that could mean anything. She gave him a grin. "No more secrets, remember?"

He cleared his throat. "It seems that Matthew Clark is angling for some kind of deal and wants to speak with me."

If she could get Clark to tell her who was after her, the threat could be defused. She'd be free to return to the mountains to have her baby. "I'm coming with you."

"Olivia, sweetheart, that isn't necessary."

But it was a risk she was willing to take.

Her mother came into the foyer from the kitchen. The worried expression on her face was a clear indication that she'd been eavesdropping. Once a spy, always a spy.

"It's not safe," her mother said. "Remember what happened last night when you followed Clark? You nearly got blown up."

"This isn't the same thing, Mom. The facility where Clark is being held is possibly the most secure site in Colorado. Armed guards all over the place. It's really safe."

She looked at her husband. "Is that right?"

Before her father could reply, Olivia was out the door with the car keys dangling from her fingers. "I'll drive."

Though her dad clearly wasn't thrilled by her company, he didn't comment as he climbed into the passenger seat and closed the door. She lowered the windows so they'd feel the breeze on this hot, summer afternoon. "Ready, Dad?"

"You're just like your mother," he mumbled. "Stubborn."

"Isn't that what you love about us? Our determination."

"Pig-headed, that's what I call it. You, your sister and your mother. All the same."

She pulled into the street and drove to the stop sign on the corner. From this vantage point, she could see the mountains west of town with the sun glistening on distant peaks while afternoon shadows glided over the foothills. A view so magnificent usually lifted her spirits, but she had too much on her plate, too much to worry about.

At the intersection, a van crossed in front of her Range Rover. Instead of proceeding forward, the van stopped. The driver turned toward them with an automatic pistol in his hand.

She ducked. Her dad did the same.

While her dad reached for the weapon in his ankle holster, a man wearing a balaclava appeared at the passenger side. He stuck his arm through the open window and fired a stun gun into her father.

Olivia screamed. She flipped into Reverse. But another car had pulled up behind them. No escape. There was no escape.

Her dad was hit. Thousands of volts of electricity charged through him. He shuddered violently and passed out in his seat.

She tried to help him, felt for his pulse at his throat. He was still alive. A shock like that could cause serious injury. He was older, susceptible to a heart attack.

Her door was ripped open. Instantly, she turned in her seat and held up her hands. "Don't use the stun gun. I'm pregnant."

"Get out of the car."

"Whatever you say."

Every fiber in her body wanted to fight, but she couldn't risk it. She had to think of the baby.

The masked men whisked her toward the van that still blocked the path of the Range Rover. There wasn't any way to stop them. She wasn't even armed. All she had was the cell phone in her pocket.

They pushed her into the back of the van. She heard gunshots. As the van door closed, she glimpsed her mother down on one knee in the street with her handgun braced in front of her, firing repeatedly.

Olivia jolted as the van raced away from the intersection.

TROY CHECKED HIS wristwatch as his brother zipped onto the highway headed toward Denver International Airport.

"We're running late," Alex said.

"I guess."

Making the flight wasn't all that important to Troy. If he'd been truly motivated, he could have pulled strings and gotten private transport that would take him directly to his team on the ground. He couldn't stop thinking about what he was leaving behind. When he checked the rearview mirror, he saw nothing but traffic, an endless stream of vehicles rushing to their various destinations. *Where am I going?*

His choice was to join his team. A sense of duty and responsibility dictated his decision, but it was more than that. To be sure, his team might benefit from his expertise, especially when it came to dealing with the other intelligence agencies involved. His knowledge of terrorist activity and strategy might also be useful. But that wasn't why he was on the road. Loyalty was what drove him. The men on his team were his brothers. If they were in danger, he needed to be there.

What about Olivia? How the hell could he leave her? Even if she couldn't admit it, the woman needed him.

"You can still change your mind," Alex said. "I can get off at the next exit and take you back to her sister's house."

"Is that where you think I should go?"

"It depends. Are you a soldier or a father?"

"Both." One occupation didn't exclude the other. "There's no reason why I can't be a daddy and a marine."

"What's your priority? In my professional opinion, Olivia looks like she's ready to give birth. It'd be a shame for you to miss that."

"Not being a medical person," Troy said, "I'm not so enthused about the hospital part. When Olivia is in labor, she's going to be in a lot of pain, right? There will be yelling and cursing, and she'll tell me that I'm a scumbag for getting her pregnant."

"Olivia isn't going to freak out. She's delivered hundreds of babies. I'm guessing that she's got everything figured out, and the birth will be natural and serene."

"And gross?"

"For a guy who's been to war, you're kind of a wuss."

His brother could be a real ass. "Thanks for your opinion, macho doc."

"If you don't want to know what I think, don't ask," Alex said. "You know whether you should be with your team or with your woman. Cut to the bottom line."

Taking his feelings out of the equation, Troy balanced the odds. His men were trained, well-equipped and had each other for support. Olivia was alone. All she wanted was to get back to her mountain cabin and have her baby. He could give her that. "Turn around."

"Good choice." Alex took his hand off the steering wheel to punch his shoulder. "When do we tell Mom and Dad?"

Troy winced. His parents lived a quiet life in retirement off the coast of Oregon. For years, they had wanted a grandchild. "Don't push it. I can still change my mind."

His cell phone rang. The caller ID showed it was Olivia. Happily, he answered. “Miss me?”

“Excuse me.” She sounded far away. There was a lot of background noise. “Where are you taking me?”

Someone answered her in a low growl. “Shut up, bitch.”

Troy sat up straight. Adrenaline shot through his veins. Olivia was being taken somewhere. She’d been abducted.

Olivia spoke again. “I want to thank you gentlemen for not hurting me. Can’t you tell me where we’re going? It seems like we’re headed east.”

Again, the growl. “Knock her out.”

“I’ll be quiet,” she said. “Not another word.”

The only sound through the phone was a rumble, and then he heard a car horn. They were in a vehicle.

“What is it?” Alex asked.

“Olivia. She’s been taken.”

Troy turned off the speaker on his phone so his voice wouldn’t be transmitted. He held the phone to his ear, listening to empty air. *She’s not hurt.* Thank God, she got that message to him. If he’d thought she was injured, he would have gone ballistic.

Somehow, she’d managed to keep her phone with her. If the line stayed open, he might be able to figure out where they were taking her. It was too damn bad that he'd disabled the GPS on her cell phone.

He snapped his fingers at his brother. "Give me your cell."

Alex handed over his phone, and Troy put in a call to Olivia's father.

It was her mother who answered. Her voice was shaky. "Four men in balaclavas. Looked like mercenaries. They forced the car to stop at the corner of Bianca's block. Used a stun gun on Richard. They took her, Troy. They took my daughter."

"Is Richard all right?"

"Physically, yes."

Troy heard the catch in her voice. She was barely holding it together. "Is an investigation underway?"

"The FBI is here."

"What have you found out so far?"

"The van was abandoned in a forested area near here. They must have switched vehicles." As she talked, she became more coherent. "They appear to be professional. They're avoiding traffic cams and surveillance."

Troy heard Olivia's voice through her phone. Immediately, he disconnected the call to her mother.

Olivia said, "Are we here already? That was quick."

"I told you to shut up."

There were shuffling noises. A car door opened.

The man with the deep voice spoke again. “What’s that in your pocket? Hey, the bitch has a phone.”

Another voice responded. “Take care of it.”

The line went dead.

Chapter Seventeen

Olivia watched her phone being crushed beneath the boot heel of her captor. Her hopes for escape were being stamped out, one by one.

From the moment they'd grabbed her, she'd been poised to run. She knew her mother had time to memorize the license plate on the van, and she expected the police to be in immediate pursuit.

But her captors had driven into the forested area near her sister's house and moved her from the van into this old, battered camper attached to the back of a truck. The makeshift vehicle looked like something deer hunters might use for a weekend in the mountains. Nobody would suspect the camper of being a getaway vehicle for kidnappers.

She was in the back with two of the four men who had attacked the Range Rover. Inside the camper, they both had to stoop. The younger of these men was black, nearly as tall as Troy but half as broad. Everything about this guy was narrow, from his nose to his pointy-toed cowboy boots. The older one was white. He had a scraggly beard, a barrel chest that made his voice resonate and cruel blue eyes. He grabbed her ruined cell phone from the floor and shoved her so she was sitting on a bench against the back wall of the camper. He held the phone an inch away from her nose.

"This phone was a mistake. A real stupid move," he said. "You got any other electronics?"

"I don't have anything else." She glared up at him. "Go ahead. Frisk me."

His buddy snorted a laugh. "She could be hiding a basketball—or a basketball team—under that gut."

"You think this is funny?" The big man snarled at the skinny guy. "Kidnapping's a federal crime. If we botch this, we'll be in a federal pen."

"I get it, sir."

"Act like it."

"Yes, sir."

The military phrasing made Olivia think these guys were an organized unit. No longer part of an army, they might be mercenaries. With a shiver of horror, she remembered Troy's warnings about the vicious deeds of Hatari. These men could be terrorists. Oh, God, what did they want with her?

The bearded man turned back to her. "If you

cooperate, you won't be hurt. Your baby won't be hurt. Understand?"

Too scared to speak without having her voice quiver, she nodded.

"Don't try anything cute like you did with the phone."

Again, she bobbed her head.

"Say it," he growled.

"I'll cooperate."

He cocked his arm and threw a quick punch that glanced off her cheekbone. Her head snapped back and hit the wall of the camper. Flashes of light exploded behind her eyelids. She was dizzy but fought to stay conscious.

His face was close to hers. "That was a warning. Do what I say."

"I will."

The side of her face throbbed with bone-deep pain. Gingerly, she touched her cheek where he'd hit her. It had already begun to swell.

The back door of the camper swung open. None of the men were wearing their balaclavas, and she thought that was a bad sign. There was only one reason that they wouldn't care if she could identify them. They didn't expect her to survive.

She had only one chance, only one hope. That was Troy. He knew how to deal with this kind of threat, and he was motivated. If not to rescue her, he'd come back for their baby.

"Let's go." The thin black man took her arm. "Come with me, and be quiet."

Any thought she might have had about running or screaming for help had been knocked out of her. If she caused a problem, they might beat her or, worse, shoot her up with sedatives. She couldn't take that risk with the baby.

As she stood, she felt a reassuring kick from inside her, as though the baby was urging her to stay strong. They had to make it through this.

Outside the camper, they were inside an airplane hangar. Quickly, she looked around for someone who might notice a hugely pregnant woman being hustled across the concrete floor. She saw no one but the four men who herded her toward a black helicopter with a blue stripe on the side. They could be going anywhere, even leaving the country. She didn't know how Troy would find her. But he had to figure it out. Her life depended on him.

AT THE SECURE facility where Clark was being held, Troy accompanied Olivia's father to the interrogation cell. Clark had specifically asked to speak with Richard to verify intelligence Clark had about an espionage debacle in 1998. If Clark's information proved valuable, the CIA might cut him a deal. This meeting was supposed to be a negotiation.

But that wasn't why Troy was here. Clark's comment about knowing who was stalking Olivia was the only clue Troy had, and he needed that name.

Other leads regarding Olivia's kidnappers had dispersed like smoke from a chimney. The sedan that was left at the scene was rented under a false name. The only viable evidence from the abandoned van was a set of fingerprints belonging to a guy who had been in and out of prison twice for robbery; his whereabouts were unknown.

Thus far, the kidnappers had been lucky. If they hadn't arranged to switch cars, they would have been in trouble because the shots fired by Olivia's mom had punctured both rear tires. Though the FBI was doing extensive research on traffic cameras, the kidnappers seemed to have successfully disappeared into traffic.

The most valuable lead came from Olivia's open phone line. Before the phone went dead, she'd indicated that they had reached their destination, and it hadn't taken long to get there. That meant they were still in the Denver area. Still close.

When Troy thought of what she must be going through, an intense rage tore through him. Going after a pregnant woman was sick, disgusting and cowardly. Anyone who would do such a thing deserved worse than death. It took an effort to hold his temper in check. His woman was in danger. His son.

Entering the room where Clark was being held, Troy noticed slight but significant changes. Clark's chair behind the table had been upgraded to a more comfortable version with padding and arms. He was sipping hot liquid from a ceramic mug, and he'd changed clothes. By asking for small favors, Clark encouraged his captors to help him even more.

Richard sat in one of the chairs opposite Clark. Troy thought the two men were well matched. They were close in age and dressed in tailored perfection. Both were clearly under stress. Even after a lifetime of CIA training, Olivia's father couldn't control the throbbing pulse of a vein in his forehead.

Clark looked up at Troy. "Won't you sit down?"

"I'll stand."

"Once a marine, always—"

"This marine saved your ass."

"So I've heard," Clark said smoothly. "You were first on the scene outside my condo. I believe you took out four men with grenades and AK-47s."

Troy neither confirmed nor denied. Clark was familiar with the training and skill level required in military intelligence, special operations. He was well aware that Troy had twenty-three ways of killing him with his bare hands before anyone could stop him.

"The name," Troy said. "I want the name of Olivia's stalker."

"I might have given you the wrong impression. This individual isn't a trained operative, and I can't guarantee that he's the man you're looking for."

Troy seethed inside. This pompous old fart wanted to play games while Olivia was going through hell. Troy flexed the fingers on his right hand. His weight balanced on the balls of his feet, ready to leap across the table and rip the answer from Clark's throat.

"A bit of advice," Richard said. "Tell him what you know and do it fast."

Clark looked into Troy's eyes. What he saw must have scared him because when he picked up his mug, his hand was shaking too much to lift it to his lips.

"The man I suspect of stalking," Clark said, "isn't part of the intelligence community. He's an acquaintance of mine, a business contact. He owns an oil firm that CRG occasionally works with. I saw him a few months ago, and he was in obvious distress. On the verge of a divorce."

"Speed it up," Richard said.

"I thought I'd take advantage of his heightened tension to push through a business deal involving oil leases. Manipulation is a most useful skill for a spy or for a businessman." He gave a shaky smile and winked at Richard. "You know how it works. People like you and I are good at getting information."

"The name," Richard said.

"When he started talking, he couldn't stop. The dam broke and all his hatred and fury came gushing through. He'd lost his infant son, and he blamed the midwife. He said her name over and over: Olivia Laughton. That's why I remembered."

"Jarvis Rainer," Troy said.

"Yes."

Troy pivoted and left the room. He'd check in with Richard later. Right now, he needed to reach his brother and pay a visit to that sweet-faced lady who worked as a receptionist at the clinic—Jarvis's ex-wife, Carol.

IN THE BACK of the helicopter, Olivia sat quietly with her hands clasped over her belly. She wore earphones that muffled the whomp-whomp-whomp of the rotors. The four men and the pilot were talking and laughing, but she wasn't hooked in to their conversation.

She'd discovered a bruise on her arm from

where they'd yanked her out of the Range Rover, her cheekbone ached and she desperately had to pee. The bearded man who hit her seemed to be in charge. Bad luck for her, he didn't seem like the kind of person who would have a shred of sympathy for a pregnant lady with a squashed bladder.

The skinny black man was much kinder. In her shorts and lightweight top, she'd been shivering, and he had tossed her a windbreaker to cover herself. If anyone was going to help her, it might be him.

Through the windshield of the chopper, she saw that they were headed west toward the mountains. A vague sense of déjà vu prickled at the edge of her consciousness. There was something she needed to remember. She closed her eyes, waiting for the nascent memory to complete itself.

When she'd been seven years old and kidnapped, she'd felt angry and helpless but not really afraid. Her mother had been with her. As a child, Olivia had believed that her mother was an all-powerful being who could prevent anything terrible from happening to her.

As an adult, she knew better. Her kidnappers were terrorists or mercenaries who couldn't care less if she lived or died. They were paid killers, and she was deeply frightened of what they might do.

The chopper took a sudden bump. Jostling in her seat, she remembered.

Her eyelids flew open. She'd been in this very helicopter before. The noise of the rotors was a heartbeat that she'd never forget. She stared at a small crack at the edge of the window. She'd seen it before. A metallic smell hit her nostrils.

The last time she'd been in this chopper, there had been another stink. The smell of blood.

She remembered Carol lying on the floor, unconscious with her broken ankle twisted at an unnatural angle. In her hands, Olivia held the limp body of the tiny infant. She'd rubbed at his back, pressed his rib cage, breathed into his mouth.

About to give up, she'd thought she saw movement from his hand. And she'd redoubled her efforts. Nothing she did had the slightest effect, but how could she quit? How could she give up this fight?

In nightmare memory, she saw the red, furious face of the baby's father. Spit gathered at the corner of his mouth. His eyes were red as fire, and he screamed at her. "You killed him. You killed my son."

She didn't defend herself. What was the point of making excuses? The baby was gone, and none of them would ever be the same.

A tear slid down her cheek. She knew exactly what had happened to her. Her kidnapping had nothing to do with Troy's terrorist cell or her parents' CIA contacts. She'd been stalked and abducted by Jarvis Rainer. And he would want his revenge.

Chapter Eighteen

At sunset, the skies over the mountains were on fire with streaks of red, yellow and gold. The furious light suited Troy's attitude. He was angry with himself for leaving Olivia unguarded and vulnerable to the approach of a madman.

He took minor solace in the fact that Jarvis hadn't harmed her. In the open-line call from her cell phone, she'd said that she hadn't been hurt. Not yet, anyway. What did Jarvis Rainer want from her?

His brother parked at the curb in front of Carol Rainer's home in the Cherry Creek district. The stucco two-story was small but elegant with a red tile entryway. A light shone through the front window.

"Nice place," Alex said. "I didn't know Carol was rich enough to live in this area."

His brother was book smart but not so clever when it came to reading people. "You know she's got the hots for you, right?"

"You think?"

"I was only with her for a couple of minutes, and she was gushing about your smile."

"Nice." Alex nodded. "Let me do the talking."

"Negative," Troy responded. "Until I know I can trust her, Carol Rainer is a suspect."

"Which is why I should handle this conversation. I happen to like this woman and appreciate the volunteer work she does at the clinic. I don't want you to scare her."

"What?" Troy didn't have time for sensitivity.

"Seriously?" His brother's eyebrows arched. "You look like you want to kill something."

"It's because I do."

And if Carol had anything to do with the abduction, Troy wouldn't hesitate before applying extreme pressure. Olivia had been missing for four hours, and every passing minute was another dagger to his heart.

Carol opened the front door before they rang the bell. In her home, she gave off a different impression than when he'd met her at the clinic. When Carol had talked with Olivia, she seemed friendly and cute with a sprinkle of freckles across her nose. The freckles were still there, but Carol had transformed into a woman who had once been married to a very wealthy man. Her long, auburn hair was carefully combed and shiny. Her matching shorts and top were raw silk.

A diamond tennis bracelet circled her wrist, and she held a wineglass in her right hand.

"Alex? Troy?" She appeared to be honestly surprised. "Why are you here?"

"May we come in?" Alex asked.

She held the door open, and they stepped inside. The Southwestern design in the interior complemented the stucco outside. Troy had the sense that the furnishings were top-of-the-line, but there was nothing pretentious in the way she'd decorated. Native American pottery in varying sizes and shapes were displayed around the comfortable living room.

He looked back at Carol and noticed the scars on her legs from surgeries following the accident nine months ago. In spite of her raw silk clothing and diamond bracelet, she was wearing rubber flip-flops with a frog design. Damn it, he hadn't wanted to like this woman. He might need to be hard on her.

Her expression showed concerned. "Is something wrong at the clinic?"

Alex took the wineglass from her hand and set it on a coaster on the coffee table. "It's Olivia. She's been kidnapped."

Troy groaned inwardly. If that was his brother's idea of a sensitive bedside manner, Alex had a lot of work to do.

Carol sank onto the sofa. "Kidnapped? Why? I don't understand."

Alex sat beside her. "Somebody has been stalking Olivia for days. Troy was here to protect her, and he thought the person who was after her might be part of a terrorist—"

"Stop." Alex was digging a hole he'd have a hard time climbing out of. Carol didn't need to know the details. "We have reason to believe your husband was behind the abduction."

"Jarvis?" Her hands twisted nervously on her lap. "He blamed Olivia. And he blamed me. According to him, our son's death was everybody else's fault."

"You don't seem too surprised," Troy said.

She snatched her wineglass from the table and drained it. "Kidnapping seems over the top, even for him. But no, I'm not shocked."

She rose from the sofa. "Would you care for wine? I need to open another bottle."

"We need your help." Alex said. "We need to figure out where Jarvis is holding Olivia."

"How would I know?"

She turned on her heel and stalked from the room. Before she made it to the kitchen, Troy was in front of her. "You're going to stay sober, Carol, because you're our only clue, our only possible source of information. I need to find Olivia before Jarvis hurts her."

Shuddering, she shook her head. "Poor Olivia. How could he do something like this?"

"You tell me." Troy led her back to the sofa. "She was grabbed by four men who appeared to be mercenaries. They drove away in a van and almost immediately switched vehicles. The operation was slick and professional. Does your husband employ men like that?"

"Not in this country," she said as she sat beside Alex again. "When we traveled in the Middle East, we had professional bodyguards and drivers. They were thugs, scary."

Good to know. Because of his work, Jarvis had access to mercenaries. And he had the wealth to pay them. A rich man with a grudge made a dangerous adversary.

"But he didn't have a regular bodyguard?" Alex asked.

"You should check with his vice president in charge of operations for Rainer Oil. He'll have a current list of employees."

Troy had already decided not to go that route. He knew what happened when the FBI and SWAT teams got involved in hostage negotiations. Olivia could end up in the center of a bloodbath. "We don't want to talk to anyone who might notify Jarvis. It's better if he thinks he got away with it."

"I don't know what I can tell you."

Alex took her hand. "I'm sorry, Carol. This is hard for you."

"I don't know what to think. Jarvis has always been childish. When we were first married, I thought his whims were kind of adorable. But when he didn't get his own way, he'd throw tantrums and sulk." She gazed deeply into his brother's eyes. "You must think I'm crazy for staying with a man like that."

"I think you're brave," Alex said gently. "You've been through a lot."

"Jarvis never actually hit me, but he was violent. At the clinic when I see abused women, I know what they're going through."

Troy watched as their budding attraction started to flower. Very sweet, but this wasn't the time for Alex to start romancing a new girlfriend.

"Carol," Troy snapped. "Concentrate."

She sat up straight. "What do you need?"

"We think he might be holding Olivia somewhere in Denver. Any ideas?"

"We had a house in town," she said, "but it's up for sale. As soon as I filed for divorce, Jarvis started unloading property. His company owns a luxury loft, but it's not the kind of place that lends itself to a kidnapper's hideout."

Troy pulled a street map from his pocket and spread it out on the coffee table. A dot in the center represented Bianca's house in south Denver. A wide circle surrounded the dot. "From the time Olivia was taken and the last communication we had from her, they could have gone this far in any direction."

Carol glanced and immediately pointed. "There. That's the airfield where Jarvis hangars his plane and his helicopter."

A plane and a chopper? The blood drained from Troy's face. How would he find her? They could have taken Olivia anywhere.

AT MCGUIRE AIRFIELD south of Denver, Troy learned that Jarvis Rainer's plane was still in the hangar, but the chopper had taken off earlier this afternoon. The timing roughly coincided with Olivia's phone call.

Since the chopper pilot didn't file a flight plan, he probably wasn't headed to a regular airport. Most likely, he was on his way to Rainer's hangar near Dillon.

Outside the flight center, lights illuminated the tarmac. Troy strode toward his brother and Carol, who had changed into jeans and a T-shirt that made her look cute again. The two of them stood under a light and chatted in hesitant bursts as though they were aware of the gravity of the situation but couldn't help the chemistry that was growing between them. Apparently, Alex had worked with this woman for weeks and barely noticed her. Now, he was infatuated. That was typical for his brother. Alex had always been shy with the ladies.

Troy spoke to Carol. "Can you find out if the chopper landed at the usual place in Dillon?"

She took out her cell phone. "There's someone I can call. Don't worry. I'll be careful not to let them know what we're up to."

While she made her call, he pulled Alex to the side. "I'm chartering a flight to go after the chopper."

"What can I do?"

In normal circumstances, he would never bring his doctor brother anywhere near danger. Troy normally worked with a team of highly trained marines who were capable of soundlessly penetrating enemy cover and defending themselves against overwhelming odds. The closest Alex had been to combat was playing video games.

"This needs to be a stealth mission," Troy said. "I want to get in, rescue Olivia and get out without Jarvis and his men noticing."

Alex bobbed his head. "Got it."

"But I'm going to need backup."

"Me? You want me to be back you up? To carry a gun?"

"Hell, no. You'd shoot your foot off."

"I'm glad we're on the same page," Alex said. "I haven't fired a gun in ten years."

"The only equipment you need to operate is a cell phone. And I think we should bring your girlfriend with us."

"Carol?" A goofy grin spread across his face. "Why should we bring her?"

Though Carol seemed to despise her almost ex-husband as much as Troy did, he didn't trust her a hundred percent not to have a change of heart. There was a time when she had cared for Jarvis, and she might not want to see him hurt.

Troy decided not to mention those doubts to Alex, plus he had another reason for wanting Carol along for the ride. "She knows her husband—where he goes and what he likes to do. If anybody can find where a man is hiding, it's his ex-wife."

Carol returned. "The chopper is there. It's an unmanned hangar, and nobody saw them land. They can't say if Olivia is with them or not."

"There's something else I need to know," Troy said. "Can you find out if your husband is at your house in Dillon?"

"Absolutely." Her grin was mischievous. "The little old lady who lives down the hill from our house hates Jarvis. She'll be happy to help me, especially if she thinks it's going to irritate him."

"Your ex doesn't have a lot of friends," Alex said.

She shrugged. "You reap what you sow. He's not a nice man."

"He never deserved a woman as wonderful as you."

She blushed. Alex took her hand. And Troy thought he might pass out from an overdose of saccharine. Carol and Alex were sticky sweet together. As far as Troy was concerned, his relationship with Olivia was a lot healthier—sometimes sour, sometimes sugar, but always tasty.

He went to charter a chopper for them to make the trip to Dillon. While the pilot was taking his credit card and information, he put through a call to Olivia's father.

Richard answered on the first ring. "Where are you?"

"I've got a good lead that I'm following. What's going on with the rest of the investigation?"

"Nothing." His voice was low. "I did as you suggested. I haven't spoken to the FBI or anybody else about Jarvis Rainer."

If Jarvis didn't know they were coming, Troy had the advantage of surprise. "Is there someone you can trust to put together an assault team? Someone who will do what you say without demanding to know why?"

"Yes."

"When I get Olivia away from her captors, I'll need backup to move in on Jarvis and his men. I don't know the exact location, but it's in the mountains near Dillon."

"I'll get the men in place," Richard said. "What kind of force are we dealing with?"

"It's the four guys who grabbed you, maybe the pilot who flew the chopper, and Jarvis. My guess is that these guys are mercenaries and should be taken as a serious threat."

"So are my guys," Richard said. "How will we know when it's time to make our move?"

"My brother will call you. You're the contact."

"Consider it done," Richard said. "I trust you, Troy. Bring my girl back."

"Yes, sir."

In the hangar, he sat back and waited for the pilot to file his paperwork and prep his aircraft. When Troy was running a mission, these arrangements were usually made by Nelson or one of the other guys on the team. They handled logistics while he mapped out the overall strategy. He missed their support.

And wasn't that ironic. While Olivia was being snatched, he had been on his way to help his team. It had been Troy riding to the rescue, thinking they needed him to pull off their mission in New York, imagining they couldn't do it without him. In truth, they were all heroes—every man on his team, every soldier in the field, every cop, every person who fought to protect the innocent.

This would be Troy's last and most important mission. He would not fail.

Chapter Nineteen

In a corner bedroom on the second floor of an old but well-maintained hunting lodge, Olivia paced from the window to the bathroom to the bed. She had a fairly good idea of where this lodge was located. Before the sun had gone down, she'd been able to see the Cathedral Rocks west of Dillon, a favorite destination for intermediate rock climbers.

If she could get out of this locked room, she could find her way back to familiar territory. The obvious escape route was through a window, but they were locked and cross-barred. Even if they'd been wide open, she wouldn't risk dropping from this height onto the hard earth below. Plus, the men who had grabbed her were patrolling outside. They were now her jailers.

An hour ago, the skinny black guy had brought a tray of food into her room and placed it on a small, round table. Though she'd tried to chat him up, he wouldn't respond. She'd expected her dinner to be porridge or some other prison fare, but the tray held a healthy, well-balanced meal of chicken, rice and broccoli. She'd eaten every bite.

Other than the slap, she hadn't been mistreated and she couldn't understand why. These accommodations were pleasant, and she was being fed healthy food. Why? Clearly, Jarvis despised her. He'd gone to a great deal of trouble to abduct her. She was his prisoner. Her head was on the chopping block. When was the ax going to fall?

Eventually, she'd have to see him. Did she have any leverage at all? Any tools she could use for negotiation? Threats were empty. Though she was sure that Troy and her parents were working hard to rescue her, Jarvis was too crazy to be dissuaded from whatever path he was on.

Or was she the crazy person? Though she'd suspected Jarvis and knew he was wealthy enough to pull off an operation like this, she hadn't really believed that he was after her. Imagining that she was the target of international spies or terrorists seemed easier than thinking that anyone could hate her so much.

She stretched out on the bed, lying on her side. What else could she use to bargain for her freedom? Ransom wasn't an option; Jarvis was too rich. Was there something else she could trade? A promise she could make?

When she heard a key being fitted in the door

lock, she sat up on the edge of the bed. Jarvis Rainer stalked into the room. The past nine months had not been kind to him. Formerly, he'd had a golfer's tan and an erect posture with his chest puffed out like a barnyard rooster. Not anymore. His shoulders slouched, and he'd developed a pot belly. His reddish-brown hair, combed back from his forehead, was noticeably thinner, and his complexion had faded to pasty-white. There was such an intense hatred in his eyes that she could barely stand to look at him.

"Hello, Olivia." His voice was raspy. "Long time, no see."

She'd had a lot of experience dealing with people in tense situations. The main thing was not to make him angrier. "I want to thank you for dinner. You've been kind."

"My plan is to take care of you. If you need anything, knock on the door. Someone will answer."

Why? "I like to take a stroll after dinner. May I step outside for a moment?"

"There's a treadmill in the exercise room on the lower level. One of my men can escort you there."

Her instincts told her that it was wise to find out as much as she could about the lodge. Keeping her tone conversational felt creepy, but it was necessary. "This is a lovely place. I'd very much like a tour."

"And we always want to do what the midwife wants, don't we?" He went to the door. "Come with me."

In the hallway outside her room, two of the guards were waiting. She gave them a nod, as though they were civilized people sharing accommodations. She followed Jarvis and they followed her as they went to the staircase in the middle of the lodge.

"This property was developed in 1948 after World War II," Jarvis said, acting the role of a tour guide. "Tourism and skiing were just becoming popular in Colorado, and the lodge was designed as a getaway for hunters and fishermen. The initial structure was little more than a cabin with its own well. It's still standing, just over the ridge from here. The owner is thinking about developing that first cabin into a special retreat."

"So you don't own this place?"

"I'm not an idiot, Olivia. I wouldn't hold you prisoner in a place that could be traced back to me. The lodge belongs to a friend who lets me use it whenever he's out of the country."

Bad news for her. Troy might figure out that Jarvis had taken her, but he wouldn't know about the lodge. She asked, "How many rooms does it have?"

Jarvis paused at the top of the staircase and

glared at her. “You like to push people. Make snotty demands.”

“I’m just curious about the house.”

“You’re in the south wing. It has four luxury bedrooms. The other side has six. That’s where my men are staying.”

“Is there an attic?” She was thinking of places she might hide if she ever got out of her room.

“It’s just storage space over the eaves. No rooms.”

He led the way down the carved wood staircase to the first floor. The main room was huge with a giant, walk-in fireplace and lots of animal heads on the walls. There were round tables that looked like they’d be perfect for playing poker.

The furnishings were rustic, including a long, polished oak table in the dining room. But the appliances in the large kitchen were top-notch. As they toured, Jarvis kept up a narrative about the history of the place and how many famous people—including presidents and kings—had stayed here. Bragging, he seemed to enjoy himself, almost forgetting the circumstances that brought her here.

“What about the exercise room?” she asked.

He pushed open a door below the main staircase and flicked a light switch. “Down here.”

The basement wasn’t as nicely finished as the upper levels. Beyond the low-ceilinged television room at the foot of the stairs were several closed doors. Jarvis opened the first door to his right, showing her a large exercise room with a wall mirror and several pieces of equipment. She noticed high windows and assumed there were window wells outside. If she could get down here, she might be able to squeeze out.

"Anytime you want to exercise," Jarvis said, "this is the place. It's important for you to stay healthy."

She couldn't stop herself from asking, "Why?"

His thin lips pinched together. He'd been waiting for her to ask. "Isn't it obvious?"

"Not at all." She wasn't good at playing games, and her patience was gone. "Why am I here?"

"Because of your incompetence, I lost my son. When I heard you were pregnant, I knew what I must do."

Dread seeped through her. She was suddenly cold, frozen with the deepest fear a mother can experience. She knew what he wanted. "No."

"Oh, yes," he said. "The child growing in your belly is mine."

TROY HAD BEEN right about Carol. An ex-wife knew how to find her husband. At the unmanned hangar in Dillon, they spotted the helicopter that belonged to Jarvis's company. Carol's friend in the area hadn't seen the chopper land and couldn't tell them for sure that Olivia had been on board, but it was a safe assumption.

Following her directions, he and Alex drove a rented SUV along back roads to a secluded cabin with a horse barn that Carol identified as the home of her ex-husband's mistress. The lights were out, and there weren't additional vehicles. Still, Troy scoped out the surrounding area and peeked through windows.

When he returned to the SUV, Alex and Carol were locked in an embrace. He opened the back door to the SUV, and they broke apart.

"Sorry," Alex muttered.

"Don't be," Troy said. "It's nice that you two are together."

"I've been thinking," Carol said as she pushed her hair back into place. "Jarvis wouldn't go to his usual tavern because there are too many people. He needs privacy."

"Right," Troy said, "and he needs to have enough space to hold Olivia and his mercenaries."

"There's a hunting lodge he sometimes visits."

"Wouldn't a lodge have other people staying there?"

"Not this place. The owner rents it out for meetings to a limited number of clients. Otherwise, there are only a few people who stay there. The time I tracked Jarvis down at this place, he was the only one there." Her shoulders rose and fell as she shuddered. "He was sitting on the front porch with his rifle across his knees."

She directed them along back roads and switchbacks. Navigating by moonlight gave her a moment's pause; the only other time she'd been to the lodge was in daylight. But they only had to double back a couple of times.

Viewing the lodge from a distance, Troy could tell that it was occupied. The upstairs windows—probably bedrooms—were dark, but lights shone through the downstairs windows and from the front porch. Using binoculars he'd bought from the chopper pilot, he spotted armed guards on patrol.

For the first time since he'd heard that Olivia was taken, he felt a surge of hope. Finding this lodge gave him a chance to rescue her. Without a word, he gave Carol a hug.

"Thank you," he said. "You've been great."

"Anything that hurts Jarvis is okay with me." She cleared her throat. "Actually, that's not true. I'm here because of Olivia. I'm deeply ashamed that my ex-husband is responsible for taking her."

Alex clasped his arm around her. "You're a good person."

Before they started kissing again, Troy interrupted. "I want to get closer to the lodge. Alex, come with me. Carol, stay in the car."

Stealth maneuvers across rugged mountain terrain were second nature to Troy. Not so for his brother. Alex stumbled more than once, and Troy had to stop to allow his brother to get his proper footing.

Out of breath, Alex whispered, "How do you sneak around like that?"

"Practice."

"I can't take more than two steps without stubbing my toe."

"Go slowly," Troy advised. "Watch where you're placing your feet and be aware of the low-hanging branches that can hit you in the face."

"Easier said than done."

"This is what I do," Troy said. "It's not like I'd know how to remove an appendix."

Though their skill sets couldn't have been more different, the brothers shared similar motivations. They both did what they could to make the world a better and safer place.

Troy checked his wristwatch. It was after two in the morning. Typically, the best time for an assault was just before dawn, which would be approximately two and a half hours from now.

The tricky part of this mission was getting inside and rescuing Olivia before anybody started shooting. Troy wanted to get a bit closer to observe the timing on the patrols and get the layout of the two-story lodge. He needed to figure out exactly where she was being held.

Bringing Alex with him on reconnaissance wasn't absolutely necessary, but Troy appreciated having another set of eyes on the problem. His brother might notice something that escaped his attention.

Pointing to a clump of trees about fifty yards away, Troy said, "Over there. By the rocks. That's where we're going."

"Got it."

"Take your time. It's better to be quiet than fast."

He glided through the trees, finding his own path where there was none. He was glad that it was summer, and they didn't have the additional obstacle of snow to deal with. At the trees, he lay flat behind a couple of moss-covered rocks and focused his binoculars on the lodge.

Two guards were sitting in front. One was smoking. Occasionally, they'd move from one side of the house to the other or go around to the back. There wasn't a regular pattern to their route or in their timing, which made it hard to predict how to get past them.

Alex lay on the ground beside him. "What do you see?"

"One door in the front. One on the side near the garage."

"Could they be holding her in the garage?"

"Not likely," Troy said. "They're patrolling the house."

"What's your strategy?"

The details were still forming in Troy's head, but he had a general outline. "From now on, I want you to be the liaison with Olivia's dad. He's in charge of the actual assault team."

"As in a SWAT team that goes in with rifles and sniper weapons?"

"Correct. Don't worry, you and Carol will be gone before the shooting begins."

"Nice to know." Alex peeked over the rock. "So how does this work? You rescue Olivia and text me when you're clear. And I contact Olivia's dad?"

"Correct." He didn't like to think of the millions of things that could go wrong, but it was important for Alex to be aware. "If I go into the house, and you hear gunfire, call Olivia's dad and apprise him of the situation."

"The situation?" Alex raised an eyebrow. "You mean if you're dead?"

"Or injured."

Troy noticed something happening at the house. A light went on. He focused his binoculars on the corner bedroom on the second floor. Someone was awake. He couldn't tell what was happening, but he felt a change in the atmosphere that was unlike anything he'd ever experienced.

Goose bumps ran along his forearm. His throat tightened as a strange anticipation bubbled up inside him.

He saw Olivia standing at the window. She wore a man-size T-shirt that was as baggy as wings on her arms and snug across her belly. Her arms spread apart. She grasped each side of the window frame as her eyes squeezed tight.

"What the hell?" He passed the binoculars to his brother. "What's she doing?"

Alex stared until Olivia disappeared from the window. "We've got a problem."

"Yeah?" The need for action was so strong in Troy that he could barely stay still. "What?"

"From my observation," Alex said, "I'd say she was hanging on to that window frame with all her strength. She was fighting a contraction."

"A what?"

"She's in labor, Troy."

Chapter Twenty

When Olivia had gotten out of bed to go to the bathroom, her water broke. She tried to tell herself that it wasn't a big deal. Lots of women had their water break a long time before they went into labor. Maybe a day. Two days.

She couldn't have the baby now. Forget her visions of a serene labor and birth, there was something more important at stake. Jarvis meant to steal her baby. She couldn't let that happen, couldn't allow her baby to be carried off by a madman into a terrifying, uncertain future.

It was vitally important that Jarvis not know that her amniotic membrane had ruptured. He didn't expect her to go into labor for days. Using a towel from the bathroom, she swabbed the clear liquid off the floor. When she stood, she felt the first twist of a contraction.

She'd counseled hundreds of women who were about to give birth, and she'd told all of them that there weren't rules they had to follow. Every labor was unique.

But she never expected the pain of her first contraction to be so acute or so prolonged. She dropped the towel and staggered toward the window. Bracing her arms against the sides of the frame, she ground her teeth together. No matter what, she wouldn't scream. Jarvis mustn't know.

The pain faded. Breathing hard, she stepped back from the window. She didn't have a clue how long the contraction had lasted. It felt like forever but was probably only a minute or two. She finished cleaning up the fluid on the floor and hung the towel in the bathroom over the shower rod.

Once labor started, most women wanted to speed up the process, and she had lots of tips on how to do that. The only way she knew to slow down was to relax. She lay on her side in bed and took long, slow, deep breaths. *Inhale, exhale, relax.* In spite of her fears, she had to ease herself into labor, to take control of her body.

There was no clock in her bedroom, and she wasn't wearing her handy wristwatch with the stopwatch function. She tried to measure the time between the first contraction and the next. It seemed like more than ten minutes. And the pain was nowhere near as severe as the first. Her tension eased. Yes, she was in labor. But it could last for hours or even a day. By then, Troy would find her and rescue her and their baby.

She closed her eyes and continued to breathe quietly and steadily. She was an expert. She could control this birth.

While managing the pain from another contraction, she was aware of the doorknob turning. If Jarvis charged into the room, she didn't know if she could hold back her cries.

The door cracked open and quickly closed again. She heard Troy's voice. "Olivia, where are you?"

"In the bed."

He slid between the covers beside her. His body was cool from the night air, and his embrace soothed the heat of her pain. She snuggled against his chest. He was here, he was really here to save her and their son.

Her whisper was nearly inaudible. "Jarvis wants our baby. To make up for the son he lost."

"Not going to happen."

"How did you get in here?"

"We should go to the bathroom and close the door. They won't hear us."

"I'm afraid to move," she whispered. "I'm in labor."

"I know."

She had no idea how he would know that she

was about to have the baby, but she didn't question or dispute his claim. "Tell me."

His lips were so close to her ear that his breath tickled when he spoke. His quiet words slipped into her mind, joining her with him in sweet intimacy.

"I felt your labor," he said, "in a flood of anticipation that permeated every cell of my body, my mind and my heart. In that moment, I knew my life was about to change forever."

She pressed her face against his chest. Tears squeezed through her eyelids.

"Go ahead and cry," he whispered. "I can take it."

"How are we going to get out of here?"

"Not the same way I came in. I scaled a wall on the back side of the house, broke a window and slipped into a bedroom. Then I waited until the guard outside your door took a pee break. I picked the lock, and here I am."

In her condition, there would be no scaling of walls or dropping from the second story. They definitely couldn't take that path to escape, but her earlier tour of the house had given her another possible route. "There's a basement. If we can get down there, I think there might be a storm door or a window we can use."

When he nodded, the bristles on his cheek scraped against her skin, and she welcomed the sensation. He made her hope again, made her feel that there was a chance that they could survive.

"I'm going to the door. When the guard is gone, I'll give you a signal and you come to me."

She wasn't dressed for an escape. Her panties had been drenched when her water broke. But she had her shorts. And her shoes were under the bed. Lying quietly and concentrating on her breathing, she waited. In the darkness, she could just make out his form near the door. He seemed to have his ear pressed to the crack.

Minutes dripped by as slowly as molasses. Another contraction came, peaked and subsided. A regular pattern for the labor pains had not been established, and that was a good sign; she wasn't close to the final urge to push.

His whisper reached her ears. "Now."

Moving as quietly as possible, she left the bed, grabbing her shoes and shorts on the way. Outside her room, the hallway was empty. Troy took her hand and led her toward the far end, away from the main staircase. The last door at the end of the hall was nearly flush to the wall. He opened it, revealing a narrow stairwell.

As she slipped inside and he closed the door, she heard voices behind them. Two of the guards were talking about who should get the next shift and who got to sleep. Pressed tightly against Troy, she stood very still. Another labor pain arose from the small of her back. She gripped his arm with all her strength and held on.

"Breathe," he whispered in her ear. "Breathe."

Forcing a slow exhale, she got through the contraction without making a sound.

The hallway was quiet again, except for the shuffling noises of the guard outside her room settling back in his chair. Together, she and Troy descended the narrow staircase. He used the light from his cell phone for illumination. She moved carefully in her bare feet. Taking a tumble would ruin everything.

The stairwell ran all the way down to the basement. When they reached the concrete floor on the bottom, Troy opened the door and shone his light around an enclosed room that was obviously used for storage. She felt more protected in here. Taking a moment, she put on her shorts and shoes.

"What do we do next?" she asked.

"When we're safely out of the house, I use my cell phone to signal Alex. He'll contact your father and—"

"Alex is here?" She hadn't expected his doctor brother to act as backup.

"Alex and Carol. We never would have found this lodge if it hadn't been for her." He ran his hand along her back. "Your father has put together an assault team. They're in Dillon, waiting for the go-ahead to move on Jarvis."

"What happened with your men in New York?" she asked.

TROY LEANED HIS back against the basement wall and stared down at the glow from the cell phone. He hadn't spared a single thought for his team since they got to Dillon. If ever he needed a sign that his priorities had changed, this was it.

"I haven't spoken to Nelson," he said. "My team is on their own, and they can handle it. All I care about is you and our baby."

"You really mean that, don't you?"

"You're everything to me."

She collapsed into his arms, holding him tightly. Her grasp became a grip. He felt the strength of her contraction. When it subsided, he said, "That one came close on top of the other."

"I haven't been able to time how far apart they are," she said. "I wish I could tell you exactly when the baby was coming, but I don't know."

"Is that your expert opinion?"

She stifled a chuckle against his chest. "A few hours ago, I didn't think I'd laugh ever again. I wasn't even sure that I'd survive."

He wrapped her up in his arms. How the hell were they going to get out of this? They couldn't stay here. As soon as Jarvis figured out that she'd left the room, he'd tear this place apart trying to find her. Going outside wasn't much better; she couldn't make any kind of long-distance run through the forest.

"I have an idea," she whispered.

"Good, because I'm fresh out."

"The original house that was on this property is about a hundred yards up the hill from here and over a ridge. It sounds like a ramshackle place, but it does have a well, which means running water."

"That's where we'll go." As soon as they were safe inside, he'd put through the call to Alex.

Using the cell phone light, he led her through a rabbit warren of unfinished rooms in the lodge basement. The high windows would have provided a viable escape route if she hadn't been pregnant; her belly was too unwieldy to squeeze through.

Finally, at the opposite end of the house from the staircase they'd descended, he found a room that was packed with firewood and had double doors that led up to outside.

Her contractions were coming more frequently. He waited for the next one to pass and pushed open the doors. They were free.

With his arm slung around her waist, he helped her climb through the forest. Her heavy breathing worried him. "Are you okay?"

"Not okay." She gasped and leaned against the rough trunk of a pine tree. "In labor." Another gasp. "Exhausted. Scared."

He scooped her off the ground. Pregnant Olivia wasn't a featherweight, but carrying her was easier than half dragging her up the hill. In the dark of the forest, he didn't see the house she'd said was in this direction. If he went past it, they could be wandering for hours.

Then he caught a glimpse of a trail and followed it along a ridge to the back door to the cabin. Though he would have preferred kicking down the door, Troy had to be careful not to make unnecessary noise that would alert Jarvis and his men to their escape route. He set her down, picked the lock and led her inside.

Filthy was a nice description for what they found in the old cabin. Dust an inch thick covered every horizontal surface, animal droppings scattered about the floor and cobwebs draped from the corners. Near the bathroom, he found a closed closet. Inside were sheets and towels that probably hadn't been used in years but were relatively clean.

He spread a sheet over the mattress in the bedroom for Olivia. "Lie down."

With a groan, she sank onto the bed, lying on her side. "How much longer?"

"Not much."

Using his cell phone, he sent a text to Alex. We're safe.

It was close to dawn. Oddly, his idea of staging the attack at that time had been accurate. The return message came in just a few minutes. Assault in twenty minutes.

Troy sat beside her on the bed and held up the phone so she could see. "Twenty minutes."

The thinning light of dawn filtered through the dirty window and shone full on her face. Slowly, she shook her head. "We don't have that long. This baby is coming now."

Chapter Twenty-One

The fear Troy had experienced in battle was nothing compared to Olivia's declaration. *Now. The baby is coming now.* And there was nobody but him to help. "What should I do?"

"This place is supposed to have a well. See if you can get the water running. And bring me all the sheets."

He dashed to the closet in the hall and grabbed every scrap of material, which he then deposited on the bed. She was standing, sorting through sheets and assembling a kind of nest.

"Should you be lying down?" he asked.

In answer, she flung out her arm and grasped his hand. The squeeze of her fingers was tighter than a hungry python. Her lips pressed together, and he knew she was holding back the urge to cry out. If there had been any way for him to take on her pain, he wouldn't have hesitated.

Gradually, she released. "Get the water."

In the kitchen, he found a couple of bowls in

the cabinets and stuck them under the cistern faucet on the sink. Each crank of the pump elicited a squawk. When the water finally started running, it was muddy brown. He kept cranking. Eventually, the liquid turned clear.

He carried a bowl of water back to the bedroom where she was sprawled on the bed, half-covered by an array of sheets and towels. In spite of the chill in the room, a film of sweat coated her forehead. Her blond hair was plastered to her cheeks, and she was gasping like a fish out of water. His heart went out to her. Olivia hadn't wanted her labor to be like this. A dozen times, she'd talked about how she wanted a mood of serenity and peace for the moment when their son came into the world.

"I wish it could be different," he whispered. "After all the babies you've delivered, you deserve a beautiful experience."

"This is perfect." She grabbed the front of his shirt and yanked him down onto the bed beside her. "Life is a struggle, and our son is going to be tough enough to handle anything the world throws at him."

"Okay." He tried to be encouraging. "That's one way of looking at it."

"Don't have a choice," she snapped.

"And that's another way."

"From now on, you're my coach. Take one of

these washcloths, get it damp and wipe off my forehead. You need to hold my hand and remind me of how to breathe."

How many ways were there to breathe? In his experience, gritting his teeth was the way to handle pain. "Inhale and exhale? Faster? Slower?"

"There's a pattern," she said. "I'll explain."

He listened to her instructions and did exactly what she said. For the next contractions, he held her hand and helped her breathe through them. They were setting up a rhythm, and she seemed to be calmer, definitely more in control. The process was working. *We're having this baby now.*

Daylight was growing stronger by the minute. In the light, his son would be born. He heard the first shots from the assault on the other house. Jarvis was under attack.

"Good news," he said. "Starting now, you can scream as loud as you want."

"You have no idea what that means to me."

On her next contraction, she opened her mouth and let out a yell. The sound crashed against his ears. Still, he encouraged her. "That's good."

"Damn right it is."

The yell seemed to relieve her pressure. "Next time, you can get even louder."

"And I need to keep to the pattern of breathing," she reminded him.

As he worked with her through the contractions, his admiration grew. She struggled. She fought with all her strength. And she was handling the labor, probably better than he would, and he'd been awarded a Purple Heart for battle injury. His suffering had been nothing compared to what she was going through. Every woman who had a baby should be awarded a medal for bravery and fortitude.

After a particularly fierce contraction, she lay back against the pillows, gasping. He wiped the damp cloth over her forehead. "How much longer?"

"Not much." She exhaled with repeated puffs. "It's time to push. Check the baby's progress."

"How do I do that?"

"I think you know where babies come out."

This was the next phase, the inevitable phase. Panic rushed through him. He wasn't sure he could handle this. But there wasn't a choice. At the foot of the bed, he pulled apart the sheets and separated her legs. "I see him. I see the head."

She bore down and pushed. The shout that came from her was a battle cry, and she was winning. They were winning. He didn't have time to think or to worry. The baby's head was freed. Acting on instinct, Troy helped the shoulders to slide through.

"Again," he said. "Another push."

Heroically, she put in the effort. The baby, his

son, was born. The tiny face was wet and covered in goop, but the kid was beautiful. His nose wrinkled and he made a weird snuffling noise—a cross between a cat's meow and a sneeze.

Troy had never been so proud or so amazed. *This is my son.* His life was forever connected to this small, helpless infant. His son. Nothing in the world had ever been so important.

Olivia held out her arms, and he nestled the baby against her breasts. After her exertions, she was a mess. Sweat dampened her tangled hair. Her complexion was red, even her eyes were bloodshot. She had never looked more beautiful.

Sitting on the bed beside his new family, he wrapped them both in a firm embrace. "You did good."

"We did good," she said.

He lightly kissed her lips. "He's perfect."

"Did you expect anything less?" Her eyelids drooped. "We're not really done. There's still the afterbirth. That's pretty messy."

"What can I do?"

"You're on cleanup duty. Remember that water you brought in here? This little guy needs to get wiped down."

Following her instructions, he took care of everything. He wiped and swabbed and changed the sheets. When it was over, Olivia sat up in the bed, holding the baby in her arms and cooing softly.

His son had a full head of dark brown hair but his eyes were blue like his mother's. He stared at the window.

"Can he tell what he's looking at?"

"I think so," she said. "I think babies are born with all the wisdom of the world, pure wisdom without language. They know every truth."

She smiled up at him. This was the serenity she'd been seeking. Down the hill, the gun battle continued. But in this cabin, the dawn light welcomed a new life.

He picked up his cell phone and put through a call to Nelson. "What's up?"

"We got them," Nelson said. "The Hatari cell is all rounded up, and it didn't take a single gunshot."

"Good job," Troy said. "Now it's your turn to congratulate me. I'm a daddy."

Nelson let out a whoop as he announced the good news to the rest of the men on his team. When they shouted their congratulations through the phone, he held it so Olivia could hear.

He said his goodbye and set down the phone on the dusty bedside table beside his gun.

"There's one more thing you need to do," she said. "Find a rubber band or a piece of string to clamp off the umbilical cord. Then you need to cut it. Do you have a sharp knife?"

He took a spring-loaded blade, standard equipment for a marine, from his pocket. "Will this do?"

"It's weirdly appropriate."

He cut a scrap from one of the sheets and used it to tie off the cord. "We still don't have a name for this little guy."

"I like Sam," she said. "Not Samuel, but Sam. Doesn't he look like a Sam?"

If she'd wanted to name him Aloysius, he would have agreed. His love for Olivia and their son was overflowing. As far as he was concerned, she could do no wrong. "Sam sounds good to me."

The shooting from down the hill seemed to be slowing down. Soon, Troy could call her father and tell him where they were, but he wasn't in a rush to share these special moments. And there was one more important bit of business he needed to take care of.

From the same pocket where he'd carried his knife, he took out his wallet. Tucked in the fold was her diamond engagement ring. He held it toward her. "You told me to ask you again."

"Yes." Her eyes sparkled. "I will marry you and spend the rest of my life with you."

After all her refusals, that was so damn easy. It would have been as good if she'd said yes on the first try. "You can't back out. Sam's my witness."

"I love you, Troy."

He kissed her mouth and slipped the ring on her finger. “And I love you, too.”

Sam made his weird little noise as though he was blessing the union of his mother and father. For a moment, they nestled together.

Then Troy picked up his knife. “When I cut this thing, it doesn’t hurt him, does it?”

“Not a bit.”

His sharp blade flicked through the cord.

A crash came from the front of the cabin. Troy leaped away from the bed. In an instant, he was in the bedroom doorway. A man with a gun lurched toward him. Jarvis Rainer was making his last attempt at revenge.

But it wasn’t going to happen. Not this time.

With a feral yell, Jarvis charged toward him. Troy flung his blade. It buried up to the hilt in the other man’s chest. He fell backwards—and didn’t move.

The same knife that had cut the umbilical cord had killed their enemy. Troy retrieved his knife, picked up the dead man’s gun and returned to the bedroom.

Olivia’s eyes were wide. “What was that?”

“Nothing for you to worry about.”

His family would always be safe and secure. Troy would make sure of it.

Epilogue

Six months later, on Valentine's Day, Olivia paced back and forth in a small anteroom at the rear of a stone chapel in Denver. Though the temperature was cold and there was snow on the ground, the sun had banished the clouds from the sky. It was the perfect day for a wedding.

Sam wiggled in her arms. He was an active six-month-old, no surprise there. He could already scoot himself across the floor, and everything he touched went into his mouth. His pudgy, little fingers plucked at the lace on the front of her gown. Though she had started the weaning process, he much preferred milk from the source. When he was this close to her, he made his demands abundantly clear.

"I know you're hungry," she said as she found a bottle in the giant diaper bag that had become an essential part of her life. "Let's try some of this."

When she poked the nipple of the bottle against

Sam's lips, he squeezed his mouth shut, turned his head and made a determined grab for the real milk. The baby was as stubborn as his father.

Carol Rainer entered the room and came toward her. "Can I hold him?"

"Be my guest." She detached Sam from her arms before he tore the lace covering her breasts. "I'm guessing that he's hungry, but I can't get him to eat. Maybe he'll take some milk from you."

As soon as Carol sat in the padded Queen Anne–style chair by the window and held the bottle toward Sam, he cooed happily and latched on to the nipple. The little traitor seemed to enjoy making his mommy look unreasonable. Olivia would have been annoyed if her blue-eyed, brown-haired son hadn't been the most adorable child on earth.

Carol smiled up at her. "You look beautiful."

"This old thing?" Olivia spun in a circle, and the skirt flared. She wasn't crazy about the pastel blue color, but it was what the bride wanted for her matron of honor. "It's almost time to start. How many people are here?"

"More than you expected. This ceremony is going to be standing room only."

"And what about Alex? Is he here yet?"

"Just showed up." Carol's smile deepened. She and Alex had been dating ever since the night when Sam was born. "And he's *not* wearing scrubs."

"Can't really blame him for the scrubs," Olivia said. "That's a doctor's uniform."

"Speaking of uniforms, those four marines in their dress blues are pretty spectacular."

Olivia agreed. The marines—including Gunnery Sergeant Blaine Nelson—were from Troy's former team. They had all been reassigned to help Troy set up a mountain training base not far from where she lived in Dillon. This new facility was designed to teach survival skills to elite troops, as well as provide some very sophisticated training in computerized technology.

Establishment of the new training base meant Troy could stay here rather than relocate to Camp Lejeune, and Olivia was grateful for the arrangement. If Troy's service meant that someday she and Sam needed to move to be with him, she'd do it, of course. But she loved her mountains. With her son and a love for her husband that grew more intense with each passing day, her life was pretty wonderful.

Her sister swept into the room, closed the door and fluffed the pastel blue skirt that matched Olivia's. Bianca exhaled a sigh. "I think I'm in love."

Olivia had heard this story before. "Did your Arab prince show up?"

"Forget him," Bianca said with a wave of her hand. "I'm talking about Blaine."

"Gunny Nelson?"

"Blond hair. Great tan. An amazing butt. Why didn't you tell me that he was so beautiful?"

"Would you believe that I didn't notice?"

"Actually," Bianca said, "I would. You and Troy and Sam are such a tight little unit that you barely pay attention to anything else."

"Not true. I've gone back to work."

"And I'm thinking you might need some help taking care of this little guy." Bianca crossed the room to where Carol was sitting with Sam. "I should come and stay with you on the weekends. I'd love to spend more time with my handsome little nephew."

"And Gunny Blaine Nelson?"

"Maybe."

Again, the door opened. Troy stepped inside. Instead of his dress blues, he'd opted for a simple gray suit that had been tailored to accommodate the breadth of his shoulders. When he took off his glasses and smiled at her, his dark eyes glistened. He seemed to be more attractive every time she saw him.

"The bride and groom have arrived," he said. "They're ready to get started."

Olivia cast a worried glance toward Carol.

"Do you think Sam will be okay during the ceremony?"

"Not to worry. I'll look after him." She stood, holding the baby. "It's not every day that a kid gets to see his grandparents get married."

"Renewing their vows," Bianca said in her lawyer voice. "They're already married."

"This ceremony is for the happily ever after," Olivia said.

Renewing their commitment was an excellent way to mark a pivotal change in the lives of Richard and Sharon Laughton. They were retired from the CIA. No longer spies, they had no secrets from each other or anyone else.

Instead of walking down the aisle by herself, Olivia would be escorted by her husband. When she linked her arm with his and looked up at him, he leaned down for a kiss. Not a gentle peck on the cheek, but a serious mouth-to-mouth kiss that sent shivers through her body.

She melted against him. "You smeared my lipstick."

"That's not all I want to mess up."

"You behave," she whispered.

"Not likely."

He wasn't the sort of man who could be tamed. It was one of his best traits.

* * * * *

Be sure to pick up a copy of
MONTANA MIDWIFE
by USA TODAY *bestselling author*
Cassie Miles in November 2012.
Look for it wherever
Harlequin Intrigue books are sold!